THE KYOTO PROTOCOL

Roger G. Trow

 New Generation **Publishing**

Prologue

In the year 2050, peace had been established in most of the war-plagued arenas of war of the early 21st Century; Iran, Iraq, Afghanistan and Pakistan were finally free of the invading foreigners that had sought to impose Western-style democracies upon their societies. For their part, the Western nations decided to "let them get on with it" and proceeded to cut off all further overseas aid to them in favour of their own home needs. A period of peace and prosperity seemed a real possibility at last.

Without the inflationary budgets fuelling foreign wars and because the Chinese suddenly stopped buying up the American debt bonds, the USA was unable to service the huge debt burden incurred forty years previously. The bankruptcy of the USA was finally acknowledged and the financial markets shifted away from the once almighty Dollar to the newly stabilized Euro. The United States entered a period of severe economic depression and lost political influence.

The political leverage of the USA was taken up by China and Europe and an uneasy balance of power now existed between the new paymasters. Europe established a technological lead over China, mainly due to the British who had finally cracked the problem of cold fusion. As a result, free and abundant energy was available throughout the European Community Nations, now known as Euro Zone, but the technology was restricted to member nations only. Asia continued to be plagued by limited resources and growing populations and China eyed its neighbours' assets avariciously.

But all that was about to change. In May 2050, massive tectonic activity erupted along both the Pacific Rim of Fire and the Mid-Atlantic Ridge.

The Asian activity began with an enormous earthquake, probably magnitude eleven, on the open-ended Richter Scale. It occurred at a shallow depth of ten kilometres, with an epicentre just off the Indonesian coast. The quake was all the more destructive because of its shallowness. Similar quakes of a high order of magnitude followed within hours along the length of the entire western boundary between the Pacific Plate and the Eurasian Plate. It is supposed that the cause of the earthquakes was the release of stress as the plates collided instead of sliding smoothly past each other.

The earthquake damage was extremely severe in those cities closest to the epicentres that lay close to the coastline. The earthquakes also generated multiple, and most severe, tsunamis, because the epicentres of most of the quakes lay at the comparatively shallow depths of between ten to fifteen kilometres. The resulting multiple tsunamis then raced across the whole of the Pacific Ocean and devastated almost every coastal region that lay on the Pacific Ocean. Whole communities just simply disappeared and this was especially true along the USA's densely populated west coast where the coastal cities were completely inundated

4

and destroyed by the huge waves and sympathetic movements of the San Andreas Fault system. The devastating power of the tsunamis reached as far south as Chile.

Twenty-four hours later, along the Marianas Trench and the Mid-Atlantic Ridge, seismic activity sensors started registering signs that a major seismic event was about to occur. The U.S. Coast and Geodetic Service put out alerts that predicted there would be imminent major tectonic movements and earthquakes; they were correct. A previously unknown flume situated right under the Mid-Atlantic Ridge raised the Ridge by twenty metres, and this combined with a large slip along the Marianas Trench. This type of activity was not predicted because plate movements in this region had until now been slow and seabed levels had been steadily adjusting for centuries. It was the combination of these events that created a second series of tsunamis, which raced across the Atlantic Ocean in both easterly and westerly directions. The tidal waves generated by the Atlantic events reached a height of sixty metres upon landfall; the westerly tsunamis and waves inundated the length of the eastern seaboard of the USA, totally destroying several cities including Boston, New York and Washington, with destruction on a massive scale even as far south as Florida.

Thus in twenty-four hours, in a nightmarish, worst-case scenario, twin sets of catastrophes dismantled the industrial might of Eastern Asia and America. The effects were felt along the whole of the European Atlantic coastline too;

Ireland bore the brunt of the killer waves first, and then shortly after it was the turn of the Atlantic coasts of Portugal and France. In Northern Europe, Holland was flooded when the dykes were breached by the huge storm surge along the English Channel; flooding was widespread along the whole Atlantic coastline of Scandinavia and northern Germany. Southern Britain was also pummelled by the huge wave system and a massive bore of water raced along the Severn Estuary devastating, in particular, the cities of Cardiff, Bristol and Worcester, totally obliterating those cities. The tidal surges from both the North Sea and the English Channel, that had broken through Holland's defences, also struck London; London's Thames Barrier was simply washed away by the massive pressure of tidal waters and so London became an inland sea.

If the cost in terms of loss of human life was enormous – the new World Council estimated that perhaps three billion souls perished worldwide in direct or resulting effects of the disasters – then the cost in terms of infrastructure and social stability may have been incalculable. The world as it once was had been destroyed. The remainder of the 21st century saw a return to feudalism and geographical rivalries, except in Euro Zone.

The whole of Asia inevitably descended into political chaos, from which only China emerged as the arbiter. Within five years, there was a realignment of the Far East's political boundaries. China seized the opportunity to annex its weaker neighbours, beginning with its claim upon the province of Taiwan. The new entity became known as the East Asian Republic (known as E.A.R.) and it simply swallowed up what remained of the shattered Asian states, which included the prizes of Malaysia, Singapore, Indonesia, Japan and Korea. The Sprattley Islands oilfields were a most desired possession, but The Philippines had to stand by silently while the E.A.R. annexed them and established a permanent military garrison to protect China International Oil Corporation's exploitation of the oil. This sent a message to all of the smaller Asian nations that in this season there would be no support forthcoming from any quarter for their legitimate territorial claims over the territories, which had previously been disputed with The People's Republic of China.

Russia followed suit and its armies rolled south. They quickly regained control of both Belarus and Ukraine and the renewed Russian Federation became essentially a 'natural resources provider' to the industrial might of the rejuvenated Euro Zone, that had risen like a phoenix from the ashes of Europe. America would struggle for another twenty years to regain its industrial strength and rebuild its influence; meanwhile it was essentially Euro Zone versus E.A.R.

Europe had fared somewhat better in its reconstruction, mainly due to several important British scientific discoveries in the 2050's; but technological implementation of the new technologies was made possible through a close political partnership between Britain and the right wing parties that had arisen in Germany and

France. But it was the powerhouses of the German and French economies that assured Britain of a bright economic future. Thus in a vibrant economy that was principally beneficial solely to its member states, the Euro Zone prospered. Furthermore, Euro Zone expanded its geographical limits by annexation southward: to include the North African States of Morocco, Tunisia and Libya. Thus it gained control over the Straits of Gibraltar and access to the Black Sea, plus Libya's oil and gas fields ensured additional reserves of fossil fuels for its industries.

In the shambles which followed the Great Flood, as it came to be known in Britain, the inept response of the British Government brought about its collapse and a series of coalition governments unsuccessfully attempted to impose order. But after ten years of weak government and rampant crime and disorder, a leader arose who would impose order with an iron fist. His name was Ian McGregor and his Progress party, backed by his jackbooted thugs, The Defenders, did what many demagogues had done before; they blamed someone else for the mess. Hitler blamed the Jews; McGregor blamed the foreigners, in particular the Asian workers and Asian immigrants. In Euro Zone, similar right wing parties had formed out of the chaos of the 2050's and having a common cause and political agenda, they united to form the new government of the Euro Zone. Power was in essence shared between London Metropolis, Paris Metropolis and Euro Central, as Berlin came to be known. The other states of Euro Zone who sat on the Euro Council effectively rubber-stamped the decisions of the Big Three.

Great engineering projects were commenced throughout Euro Zone, thanks to unlimited cheap energy from the new fusion process and the development of robotics and artificial intelligence. Thanks to the success of the new partnership in research and development with German and French industries, Britain began to benefit from an inflow of great wealth; a new London began to take shape. The draining of the London basin became a priority and it was made possible through McGregor's authoritarian government. A new Thames Barrier was erected and the waters were pumped out. Old areas of London were cleared if they did not conform to the new modernistic image of the city, which was in the mind of Ian McGregor. In place of most of North London, for example, a massive construction was undertaken; the first Super Dome in the world.

In the new Super Dome it was possible to take an internal monorail to any hub without ever seeing the outside world: schools, hospitals and every social amenity were enclosed in the shiny syntho-glass and structural plastic dome. Upper levels of the dome were reserved for apartments and recreational pursuits, with high speed lateral or vertical elevators linking to the transportation hubs. A similar project was constructed in South London; McGregor deemed the old untidy aggregation that comprised London, north and south of the river, to be inefficient. It might also be said that in the new Super Domes, efficient policing was now possible; thus, in his view, he had solved the issue of inner city crime. In due course, similar projects were to be constructed for the sprawling Birmingham and Manchester Metropolis. McGregor also argued that the new Super Domes would curb the expansion of the cities into what little remained of the countryside, so to complement the Super Domes, new countryside zones were established where development was totally prohibited.

McGregor also pushed for the maglev train project to be constructed, thus linking London Metropolis, Paris Metropolis and Euro Zone Central by an efficient all-weather, high-speed transportation system. The maglev train replaced the decrepit Channel Tunnel rail link between the UK and Europe. A gigantic bridge between Dover and Calais was constructed; it carried the maglev trains, and its height permitted ocean-going vessels to pass underneath. This only became possible through the development of new lightweight, high strength plastics for structural uses.

Once again, it should be emphasized that the partnership of nations provided the positive environment that made it possible to take on such joint massive construction projects, but that combined with the new technologies had led to Euro Zone's newly gained affluence. It was the brashest advertisement of the emergence of a revitalized Europe, or as some put it "Europe on steroids!"

Chapter One: The Journey's End

The maglev train glided to a halt.

"This is London Metropolis Central," intoned the public address systems. "Please observe the immigration arrival and departure rules; all aliens must report to the Defenders' Office for registration."

In every direction around the vaulted concourse, huge public information screens flashed the latest news of train departures, arrivals and delayed connections. A never-ending stream of public propaganda messages bombarded the senses of the horde of weary travellers who disembarked the giant train. Leaping upon the walkway belts, the crowds of arriving passengers converged upon the exits, clutching their personal baggage and documents, ready to show if required at the scanner checkpoints ahead. For the most part UK citizens and Euro Zoners walked freely through the gates, having been automatically logged and scanned by the remote scanners in the concourse.

Meanwhile, like an otherworldly synchronized ballet, the army of luggage drones and ground cars converged upon the shining monster. Weaving and dancing, they loaded their cargo pods into the belly of the maglev train and its aerial storage lockers; ten thousand tons in five minutes, that's what the schedule said and The Superliner was never late, never. At midnight, the maglev train would depart, heading south, next stop Folkestone, Kent; and then, mounting the colossal Channel Bridge, it would head for Paris Metropolis and Euro Zone Central, at an average speed of three hundred and fifty kilometres per hour.

Embarking passengers passed through the ground scanners before mounting ground cars or walkway belts to their designated pods, which were to be mounted onto their connecting trains. Each pod had a designated destination, thus minimizing transfer time. When the pod had its complement of passengers, huge loading machines with extended hydraulic arms would position the pod in its designated position on the train.

The Station was fully monitored by scanners, both visible and remote scanners, security was always tight. Sniffers and dogs would monitor passengers entering and leaving the Station Precincts for drugs, weapons or explosives. All citizens were required to wear tags with a written ID and RFID, so identities could be checked both manually and remotely. All non-Euro Zone visitors wore live tags, which were colour coded to indicate the validity of their visas. Occasionally, the scanners would pick up an anomaly in the RFID's of the surging crowd. A struggle would ensue, a ripple in the tide, and the Defenders would quietly lead the malefactor away from the gates.

"What's up?" someone might ask.

"Nothing to be concerned about, sir, just another over-stayer, but we always catch 'em!" the Defenders would mechanically intone.

Since the Big Dip, there were many who wanted to share in the hard won prosperity of His Britannic Majesty's realm, but HM's Government was equally determined to curb the influx of economic migrants; "Let's keep Britain for the British!" said one of the endless slogans on the PI screens.

Seemingly oblivious to the general pandemonium all about him, a tall, brown-haired, middle-aged gentleman moved purposefully from The Superliner to his private travel pod for a connecting train. It was due to leave within fifteen minutes, and in the new local Maglev train designated for his limited stop express to Exeter the journey time should only be sixty minutes, but progress was expected to be slower than usual owing to ongoing construction and improvements along the route. He carried himself with an erect posture that reflected his military background but walked with a pronounced limp that indicated that he had seen active service; he carried in his left hand a bulging briefcase, which he'd vigorously protected from the assistance of the maglev train steward.

Dr. Jim Stewart PhD. entered the passenger pod for the Castle Cary/ Exeter Express; mercifully it would be a quiet journey home tonight on the Exeter Express, for apart from him the only other occupant of the pod was a young lady. Actually, she seemed little more than a girl in the subdued lighting of the pod. A cursory glance revealed that she was from the East Asian Republic, probably from Japan, which was most unusual to see these days, in the aftermath of the destruction of Tokyo in The Big One; and with the fall of the once mighty Yen, which Japanese could afford to travel anymore?

Stewart's curiosity was aroused and he observed her again. Her head was down and she sat hunched in a corner of the pod, by her side there were two bundles; the larger one was clearly a young child, maybe a girl, and the other smaller bundle seemed to consist of her entire luggage. Most curious! Particularly, he noted the RFID badge flash on her shoulder, it was flashing green and then orange. "Must be a relatively new visitor," he mused.

At that point Stewart chose a seat across from the girl. The passenger pod was now in place, the journey was about to begin, and evidently no more passengers would be joining them. He continued his appraisal; mid-twenties maybe, short hair in a rather light brown tone, quite unusual cut too, black leather coat to knee length, jeans and sneakers to finish it off; quaint, rather twenty-first century fashion! Nothing very unusual really, only the hair colour!

Jim Stewart was a trained observer; in his line of work it paid to never take for granted that your companion was harmless, even if she looked it. He recalled several assassins that had narrowly failed to kill him in the past, only because he had always carefully scrutinized the body language of strangers and the 'tells' that everyone had when they were pretending to be something that they weren't.

Just then she raised her head and looked at Stewart directly. He was totally unprepared for the vivid green eyes, but what came next nearly floored him.

"Dr Jim, will you help us?"

Jim Stewart was seldom floored; in fact he was known for his calm, unflappable demeanour. "Who, who are you?" he stammered, "and h-how do you know my name?"

As if he had not spoken at all, she repeated her question. "Will you help us?"

"Well, that depends upon you," said Jim, "and more precisely, upon what answers I get before we reach Castle Cary Station!"

For a moment she dropped her gaze, and then in a lower voice, she asked, "Is it safe to talk here?"

"Yes, don't worry," he replied, indicating the mobile jammer on his belt. "Never leave home without one!"

Hearing this, she relaxed, and nodded and then smiling, she said brightly, "Well, it's going to be an interesting homecoming alright!"

For the next few minutes, they shared the silence, looking from the pod window upon the myriad lights of the capital, as the Exeter Express negotiated the local links around the North London Super Dome. Jim supposed that one day they would come up with a credible alternative to 'Super Dome!' "How could such a ridiculous term be applied to a town?" "It was," he supposed, "a reflection on the ego of that megalomaniac, McGregor!" Soon they passed Woking, in a little while it would be Andover and Jim would be near his beloved West Country. It was good to be home in England, even the England of Ian McGregor. In his mind he anticipated with pleasure the green hills of Somerset, all the more as he neared home.

After a long tour of duty – first in shattered Arunachal Pradesh, India, where the former Peoples Republic of China, now E.A.R, was again raising tension; and then in Eastern Euro Zone, where the Russian Federation's starving multitudes clamoured to be admitted to the lush pastures of the Euro Zone, and attempted border infiltrations demanded constant vigilance, which was Jim's speciality – Dr. Jim Stewart was very, very tired.

The nuclear exchanges between India and Pakistan in the mid-twenty-first century had threatened to drag the whole world into a war, but by the time that calmer voices had settled the dispute, most of both northern Pakistan and India were devastated, and only now were they beginning to re-establish total sovereignty; just the sort of opportunity that the E.A.R liked to capitalize upon, as witness the annexations of Japan and Korea after the Tsunamis and Earthquake disasters in 2050. The Euro-Asian theatre was still a very volatile place and total vigilance was required in every theatre.

The Maglev train swished silently along, hovering a mere five millimetres above the power rail, the only sound being the click, click as they passed through the old local railway switches. The lights of the London Metropolis receded and the remnants of the old suburbs flicked by; soon they would be entering the Rural Zone and the bejewelled towers too would be no more.

A tear rolled slowly down the young woman's cheek, but she seemed unaware of it. She watched the city's lights pass by. Finally she whispered, "Once I lived in a city like this, but now it's gone, all gone".

Suddenly the panel above the head of the young woman glowed red; a message from London Metropolis Central, no less!

"Call for Dr Stewart, from the Cabinet Secretary's Office. Are you able to take the call now, sir?" Of course they knew exactly where he was, didn't they book his reservation? Come to think of it, wasn't he supposed to have sole occupancy of the pod? He'd have to ask the girl about that too!

"Yes," Stewart replied, "but private mode please, I'm not dressed for company!" Now why did I say that? Why did I instinctively wish to shield her? Quite strange!

"Evening Jim, sorry to bother you at this hour," the voice of Astley Sinclair boomed out, somewhat insincerely, through the pod's PA system. "I needed to run something by you." "You're very welcome," Stewart replied, just as insincerely. "Fire away!"

"I wonder whether you would be up to another sortie, this time to the Turkish Eastern Border?" Astley Sinclair continued, "You see, we have had some rather disturbing intelligence about some E.A.R. infiltrators... and while that's nothing new, it seems that these particular ones have found a way to totally evade detection by our scanners. Of course, this is your field, Jim, but we know that they must have developed some new technology… very worrying, very worrying indeed!" He concluded abruptly, "I'll send you the file, so you can skim through it; see what you can make of it all; on your day off of course!" Then with a short sharp bark, which passed for a laugh with Astley Sinclair, he was gone.

"Yes, I'll bet they're worried!" thought Jim, "that would certainly bring Fortress Europe crashing down if the 'intelligence' was correct! I can just imagine Mr High and Mighty McGregor would have an apoplectic fit at the very thought of thousands of 'foreigners' waltzing across his impregnable fortress' boundaries! Oh well, maybe I can scrape a few days off while I chew on this problem?" Jim opened his comm. device and quickly scanned the communication from Sinclair, and then on a sudden impulse, with a few keystrokes he shot off a data request to Ahmet, his company's representative, and an old friend, in Istanbul. He also attached a copy of Sinclair's data file. "Let someone else do the legwork for now," he thought.

"Now, young lady, where were we?" Jim continued, "Oh, yes! Would you begin by telling me just who you are, and then, if you please, how did you gain entrance to this secure travel pod; and finally I suppose you'd better tell me just how you believe I may help you?"

The young woman looked up at Jim again, and again that shock wave passed over him. She was actually very attractive, in a Eurasian kind of a way, and those eyes had a sort of mesmerizing effect over Jim. "Perhaps this might save a lot of discussion," she replied, and she held out a rather antique-looking chronometer watch, the sort that one only sees in museums these days. "Do you recognize it, Dr Jim?"

Jim nodded. Of course, Jim knew it instantly; one cannot forget that someone who saved your life! Slowly, Jim turned the watch over and read the inscription that he had had engraved upon the watch back; "*To Toshio, whatever and whenever, I'll have the time*".

"The man who owns this watch saved my life in Korea. I owe him a debt of gratitude that I could never repay!" Then he lowered his voice and in a menacing tone, he added, "So, just how did *you* come to have the watch of Toshio Hokaida?"

There was a brief hesitation, and then she replied, her eyes flashing, "Toshio is dead! I am Sakura, daughter of Toshio Hokaida. He died protecting my mother and me from the E.A.R. agents who stormed our home in Kyoto. The cowards could not defeat him, for he was an expert in the martial arts, but they stabbed him in the back, the scum! We fled and took refuge in the Underground Movement, but they keep looking for us because of the secret work that my parents were engaged upon. Dr Stewart, if you are indeed the great friend of my father and the man of honour that he said you are, I have come to ask you to honour your debt to my father's memory!"

Jim Stewart sat absolutely still for a long moment, but his thoughts raced. He felt so sad to learn of his dear friend's murder. Toshio was a hero several times over; many times he had gone out under fire to rescue wounded men, men like Dr Jim Stewart, when he lay bleeding to death from wounds caused by fragmentation grenades.

Finally he asked Sakura, "Do you recall what is written there; *whatever and whenever, I'll have the time*? For the daughter of Toshio Hokaida, I have the time."

"Thank you, Jim," she said quietly; and then in a brighter tone, she continued, "and now, would you like to see your daughter?"

Chapter Two: A Family Man

She turned and revealed the sleeping child, a girl of about four years of age. The child looked more European than her mother, fine brown hair tumbled across her forehead. Jim wondered whether the girl had also inherited the extraordinary eyes of her mother. "OK, so who is really the father? We never met before; I know I would remember you."

Sakura blushed and then after a moment she answered him. "I'd better begin at the beginning, as they say. My father, as you know, was a resident surgeon in the I.F. war front hospital in Incheon, Korea, an International Force volunteer like yourself. What you didn't know was that he was also a brilliant genetic scientist, as was my mother, an American, Dr Glenda Woods. My mother met you during your convalescence, but you may not recall her since you were on heavy morphine dosage during that time. Toshio and Glenda fell in love at that same hospital and they secretly worked together on the genetic research, which was the other passion that they shared. At one point Toshio feared that he was going to lose you, his closest friend, Jim; it was touch and go for a long while. And so they decided upon a rather unethical action; they would take samples of your genetic material, including semen, and somehow they would restore you. Perhaps they originally thought that it might be possible to create a clone or using stem cells grow replacement organs for those that the shells had damaged, but that proved too much of a task, given the rather rudimentary facilities in the war hospital. In the end, they stored the materials and pursued other scientific enquiries."

"When you made a welcome but unexpected recovery, they decided to say nothing further about the sampling and their experiments. By the way, our daughter's name is Grace; we felt that it was appropriate, considering her origins."

"OK, so let's say that I accept all of this; how come that suddenly your parents decided to use you as a birth incubator for this child? Why, after all these years, did they implant their own daughter with my sperm?"

Again, Sakura blushed, this time most deeply. "I am sorry, it is difficult for me to speak of these things, especially with you, and I hope you understand?" Jim nodded. His eyes searched her face, seeking for any sign of evasion. Finding none, he said, "I'm sorry too, perhaps I should be more sensitive of your feelings. I apologize again; please tell me more."

"In the course of their other research they stumbled upon a new protein, which they speculated might have some promising qualities, and so they decided to test its properties on the lab rats. What they discovered was that when the protein was simply injected into the test subjects, they appeared to have an expansion of their intelligence, which was exciting in itself; but what was mind-blowing, Jim, was that their offspring evidenced memory of the tests that the parent rats had experienced… think of it! They had discovered 'inherent memory'! After exhaustive double blind tests and testing with other populations, the protein's potential was confirmed; they dubbed it 'KP,' short for "Kyoto Protocol." The implications for this breakthrough began to sink home; in the wrong hands this might be very dangerous!" She paused for a moment, then, seeing that Jim was still attentively listening, she continued at a quicker pace.

"What they also needed to do was to see whether the KP would be effective upon human subjects, and if there would be unpredicted side effects. At first they decided to keep quiet about KP; it was a very troubled time and there was a war raging all around them. They returned to Kyoto, our home city, where they could work privately to develop their new protocol."

"They decided to self-test the KP, but the dosages were hit and miss really; but, as it turned out, this was exactly the catalyst that was required for stage two. There were some signs that KP was becoming effective in the way that they had hoped, intelligence was expanded and memory retention was significantly improved. Jim, the human brain has immense unused capacity; some estimate that we use less than ten per cent of our available brain power, and what other abilities might be released by successfully exploiting the properties of KP?"

"The E.A.R. had annexed our country, Jim, and it was vital that the research was preserved; it couldn't be allowed to fall into the enemy's hands! Eventually, because we shared DNA material already, they decided that the safest place and the best test subject for the second stage of the experiment was me; so they prepared a genetic solution containing material from both of my parents DNA with a booster of KP and it was injected into me. I was eight years old at the time. The results began to become evident within a short while; in my case, it was only two weeks before we started to see some results within the predictable parameters."

"You may also have noticed the rather intense colour of my eyes?" Jim nodded silently. "That was one of the unpredicted side-effects of the KP, it seems to impart an intense pigmentation to the natural colour of the subject's iris. From the age of eight, I have been developing my mental abilities. I now speak ten languages, from my parents I have acquired an expert level ability in genetics and science; and there are certain intuitive abilities, but I would say I come short of being what you would call a telepath."

"Wow!" Jim exclaimed. "Where do I get my shot?" On a more serious note, he continued, "I can see that this protein has had a profound effect upon you, simply from an injection into an eight year old. But surely, if KP was introduced into an embryonic foetus, wouldn't there be even more changes observable? I am not a geneticist, as you know, but clearly this KP is interacting with and modifying the DNA of the host, and it seems to me that the assimilation of KP by the foetus must initiate a whole new development cycle?"

"Yes, you are absolutely correct," Sakura replied, nodding emphatically. "Grace is a special child, I would go so far as to say that she is E. Homo-sapiens; E stands for 'enhanced'! Grace can already do some pretty amazing things. Instinctively, she understands much more than she can speak and it is certain that she is a natural telepath, with abilities still developing".

She continued her narrative. "They continued to live and work in Kyoto for fifteen more years and for the most part the E.A.R. left them alone. However, it was becoming increasingly difficult to conceal my mother's presence because of her Caucasian appearance. It was only a matter of time before she would be picked up and interrogated about her research, so that was why they decided to inseminate me with your semen and a further booster of KP; in this way the KP would be saved and the effects upon an embryonic transfer could be monitored; they fully expected a more powerful reaction. It was four years ago that Grace was born."

"Oh, by the way; as a security measure, my parents also inseminated two other KP-enhanced embryos into two surrogate Japanese mothers. Both are close cousins of mine, named Asuka and Ren, so actually there are two other children just like her. So overnight, Dr Jim, you have become the father of triplets!"

"Wow! Well, I think that is quite enough for me to take in for now!" said Jim. "Why don't you rest for a while? I have to arrange our reception at Castle Cary; we shall be arriving within the hour;

the ground car that I left at the station won't be so convenient for us all. I'll just place a call to my brother to ask for the rotor vehicle to come to the station."

"Bill, hi! Sorry for the late call. Do you mind sending down the chopper to meet me at the station? We have two unexpected guests, a woman and a child, I'll fill you in later on the details... yes, they can stay in my cottage, and I'll find room for us all... and, Bill? Would you just keep this between us for now? You can tell John, of course. I think we need to be discreet on this one, if you know what I mean?"

He closed the comms device and, as if reading the unasked question in her eyes, he said, "It is a secure link, engineered it myself. Not even the Defenders can scan my calls!" That said, Jim settled down on the other bench seat. Perhaps he might rest, but sleep was impossible now, with his thoughts racing back and forth... the I.F. Hospital at Incheon, the girl with the green eyes, and what about these super-kids! What a homecoming, indeed!

Again the pod's screen sounded for an incoming call. Jim switched off the visual once more before answering. It was Major Hinckley, of the Defenders Surveillance Department. "Hello, sir; my apologies for the late night interruption. We have a security alert on all trains exiting London Metro Central this evening."

"Really?" asked Jim with a sinking feeling in his stomach. "What's up?"

"Well, sir, it appears that there is an anomaly in the head count at London Metropolitan Central."

Jim interrupted Hinckley's explanation. "Major, as you well know, there are often anomalies; people get lost and miss a train, why, we have even had people die on the platform! Have you eliminated all of the usual causes?"

"Yes sir, indeed we have," Major Hinckley replied stiffly, "and we know our job, Dr Stewart. It has now become necessary to do physical inspections of every train that left London Metro in the past hour. Kindly cooperate with the Defenders who will board your pod at Andover. We will merely be checking the ID's of all passengers; we don't expect it to seriously delay you, sir."

Jim closed the channel. The Defenders were very much a law unto themselves and the deference given to Jim was solely because of his vital role in security matters, but both he and the Major knew very well that Jim did not have the power to countermand the search. He had absolutely no idea how he would explain their presence in a secure pod for starters. It looked like they were all going to be in trouble, him too, for harbouring fugitives apparently… it seemed that Sakura and Grace would be exposed and there was nothing that he could do about it.

He turned to look at Sakura. She merely smiled and said, "Nothing to worry about, Dr Jim! How do you suppose that we got this far?"

Jim's comm. link sounded again. A new message was coming in from one of Jim's informants; more new data about another infiltration in Germany as well as more details of the first one, which was reported in Turkey. In both cases the Euro Zone's border patrols had butchered all but one of the infiltrators, who had escaped; that smacked of the heavy hand of Deputy Director of Operations, Wolf Braun. The man was noted for his ruthlessness; in the East on the Russian Border, four persons had died and in the Turkish border incident another nine had died. The files included full site intel, and to Jim's keen mind there was a pattern linking the two infiltrations. Anyone with half a brain could have seen the benefit of taking the infiltrators alive, but sometimes Wolf's men were just too trigger-happy! Jim transferred both data files to his home network for further study tomorrow.

Within a few minutes the train began to slow and then came to an abrupt halt; the sounds of a search filtered into the passenger pod. Voices were raised and screams were heard from the adjoining pod, followed by the sound of crying women which confirmed Jim's worst fears about the manner in which the search was being conducted. In a few moments, his pod's door was activated and two Defenders entered.

"Your ID please, sir?" the leading official asked. "Has anyone else entered this pod since you left London?"

"Well, this pod is sealed, as you well know," replied Jim. "How could anyone enter?"

"Quite so," the Defender replied. "Sorry to have disturbed you, Dr Stewart." The Defenders

28

left quietly, relocking the pod with their security key.

In a few more minutes, perhaps ten, the search was complete and the train was able to resume the journey.

Jim looked at Sakura in amazement. "What just happened?" Grace was sitting up on her mother's knee, her eyes open, a deep blue colour.

"Grace protected us. They never even saw us," she replied. Suddenly, Jim understood the connection between the three children and the mysterious infiltrators... yes, the footprints found at the two scenes had been small, but probably adult; the weight impressions, however, indicated that both persons had been carrying a load. The obvious conclusion was that they were both females carrying infants. It seemed clear now that Jim's children were converging upon Europe, but for what reason he could not tell.

Chapter Three: Lessons in Humility

The Bee Hive, or The Hive for short, was an imposing edifice of golden syntho-glass and burnished alloy panelling with a high tensile plastic frame within. Standing sixty stories high, on the banks of the River Thames and overlooking Old London and the New Districts, it epitomized everything about the Progress Party and its leadership, particularly Ian McGregor. It was brash and somehow vulgar; even though only the best architects and finest designers had been permitted to submit their proposals, somehow whatever came out of the Progress Party's designs always seemed to be, well, tacky.

Ian McGregor stood before the panoramic windows of his office, which was on the sixtieth floor, naturally. McGregor's office was uncharacteristically in the style of the mid-eighteenth Century; his desk was of mahogany in the Chippendale style and was matched with exquisite original Chippendale chairs. All of the furniture in the office was in mahogany, but low profile, so as to not spoil his view of the city. He affected to be the consummate image of the new leader; his suits were impeccably tailored by London's finest bespoke tailor, Samuel Smith, his shoes were handmade, as were his shirts. "It's all about image," McGregor was fond of saying, and indeed that carried over into his political life also. He conveyed the image of the most successful, powerful and visionary leader of the twenty-second century. Only he knew that in his dreams, he was still the upstart from Glasgow, in his youth wielding both a club and a razor to claw his way out of the ghettos. One of his first projects as Leader of the ruling Progress Party, Prime Minister of Britain and de-facto dictator, was to level the entire neighbourhood where he had grown up; a green park now graced the site of the city's former most notorious slum.

He had a three hundred and sixty five degree view over the London Metropolis area. On every side, brash new buildings competed for the sky. London was a boom town; redevelopment shouted "Progress!" except in the Old Town, which – except for the flood damage – was largely unchanged in its early twenty-first century splendour. This assuaged his conscience; good for the tourists, he supposed.

Far below and to his right, he could see the crumbling monument that was Buckingham Palace. Only His Britannic Majesty, King Charles the Fourth, dwelt there now; as irrelevant as his domicile in the modern world. Oh, on paper Britain was still a constitutional monarchy, but everyone knew that old 'C Four' was just that; barely able to mumble his way through the occasional prepared speech at a Progress Party State Dinner for a visiting functionary from the E.A.R. or elsewhere. Totally irrelevant! But it seemed to McGregor that he was being kind to the old duffer; after all, he was well provided for, as long as he toed the line of course! For McGregor that line was unambiguous, in the old phrase of the twentieth century; "My way or the highway!"

"People didn't want to be confused," he told himself, and whoever else that would listen. "Too many choices lead to confusion, which leads to a lack of direction and ultimately to a lack of a government!" McGregor's lack of remorse for his part in the public rioting that led ultimately to his predecessor's demise and his own meteoric rise to power twenty years ago, were characteristic of the man and his sense of destiny justified his own lack of ethical standards, right up to the present day.

He was expecting a visitor, at this late hour. McGregor's stamina was legendary and he expected everyone else to work the hours that suited him.

The visitor arrived. John Sanford, Minister of Public Security, was arguably the second most powerful man in Britain. He oversaw the internal security and surveillance apparatus; the Public Defenders were his men, to a man. Every international entry point, every internal transit point and just about every street corner were under his scanners. Rumour had it that, in the new Super Domes of North and South London, every apartment was monitored by hidden cameras and microphones; the rumour might well have been true! People disappeared quietly in Britain, especially those who voiced open criticism of the Progress Party, and John Sanford knew where all the bodies were buried.

Today the two men were meeting privately to discuss the issue just brought before Dr Jim

Stewart by Astley Sinclair. Sanford began his report in his usual direct manner.

"We have reliable intelligence, supported by other independent sources, that the E.A.R. has found a way to avoid our scanners on the Turkish border. Ten persons were observed initially by a mobile scanner unit inside the security zone; that was three days ago; but then the equipment appeared to malfunction and we could only see nine persons. A follow-up mission was initiated by the local commander using a rotor-turbo vehicle, but the aerial observers could only see the nine persons shown on the second scan. A ground patrol subsequently observed ten sets of footprints at the site of the original border crossing, but the tracks of the tenth person who had diverged from the main party became difficult to follow, owing to the difficult terrain. After a chase of approximately thirty minutes, we located the main group of infiltrators and in the ensuing resistance all nine persons died 'resisting arrest'. No trace was ever found again of the tenth person. The Turkish authorities continued to sweep the area for the next forty-eight hours, but no other sightings have been made. The bodies of the infiltrators, upon examination, proved to be Asian; all males, and they wore E.A.R. desert boots. It is suspected that they were smugglers, as the border there is rather prone to this type of activity."

"What were the other independent sources that you mentioned?" asked McGregor in his usual incisive manner, "and why are we bringing up this issue at this level; surely this matter is for your technical people to investigate?"

"Yes, sir," Sanford replied. "Indeed, we have one of our best experts working on it right now, as we speak. But the sources to which I make reference are credible intelligence operatives that we have embedded in the E.A.R. government. They have warned us that there are certain disaffected elements in their security forces that have removed a vital weapon from the Province of Japan. We don't know the nature of the weapon; whether biological, tactical nuclear or what; but this we do note, the E.A.R. are mobilizing and we hear that they believe that there is a person unaccounted for in the Turkish border incident.

"Well," McGregor replied, "you know with the Russian Trade talks coming up next week, we certainly don't want any other dramas that might cloud the issues." He continued, "the Russians need our energy desperately now, and we need their minerals. It's a marriage made in Heaven, let's not screw it up!"

With that dismissal, Sanford left as silently as he had arrived. McGregor stood brooding over his beloved view as the anger began to build in him. Finally he kicked out at the nearest object, which happened to be one of the Chippendale chairs. The chair flew across the office, eventually landing against a distant wall minus one of its Cabriole legs.

"Damn, damn and damn again!" he muttered. Finally, his calm restored, he picked up his phone and spoke quietly to his secretary. "Send a signal to Wolf Braun, in Euro Central, and attach a copy of Sanford's report. I'd like his feedback on this matter!"

Meanwhile, in Istanbul, Gabriel Aoun sat alone in his nightclub. Before him an empty bottle of Scotch whisky, but Gabriel's head was crystal clear, as always. His eyes constantly roved the club, noting the big spenders, the unruly drunks who might have to be ejected but he especially noted those who sat quietly in the darkened corners. These last were often the best customers for Gabriel, but sometimes they could be trouble too. His gun nestled quietly on his lap, just in case.

The club was full of girls as usual and many foreigners came looking for the Russian girls that Gabriel provided. The Russians loved to dance and did so with reckless abandon, their short skirts flying high as they did the bump and grind to the heavy beat of the nightclub's band. In the back of the club, there were rooms for the use of his favoured customers. They would be entertained by the Russian girls into the small hours, sometimes two or three girls for a client, but only if they had been lavish spenders that night. Gabriel didn't play favourites; it was all about money.

Gabriel really had only one pet beef, and that was a total taboo on drugs; no one could bring them in, sell them or buy them in his club. Gabriel was pragmatic; drugs eventually spoiled the girl, which means his investment becomes tarnished; it was good business to 'say no to drugs', as all the posters warned.

Wherever there was booze, gambling, girls and men with a thirst for all of these, there would be a free flow of information, which was Gabriel's specialty. Gabriel was, you see, a broker. He dealt in anything commercial, except drugs. As a Christian Lebanese in a Muslim country, he was a minority whichever way you looked at it, and this taught one to be shrewd and cunning, not to mention resourceful; and Gabriel Aoun was all of these.

A man who had been sitting quietly sipping his drink at a corner table rose and made his way across to Gabriel's table. He was dark-skinned, probably Kurdish. He spoke with a Turkish accent anyway.

"Gabriel, someone told me that you are a broker in many things."

"Indeed," replied Gabriel, "but who might this someone be that told you this?"

"He said to tell you only, 'J.S.' sent me."

The initials brought a sense of anticipation to Gabriel. Surely this was going to be a profitable venture! "And what did J.S. want me to hear?" Gabriel added.

"Not to hear, to read," the stranger replied, as he passed an envelope containing a data crystal across the table.

Gabriel slipped the crystal into his reader. After perusing the contents thoroughly, Gabriel said simply, "I will see what I can do; give me twenty four hours and come to me here. But bring money next time, J.S. knows my rates!"

Astley Sinclair was having a very poor night. Just as he was getting into his REM sleep phase, there was a shrill alarm as a top priority signal burst in upon his slumber. Beside him the teenaged blonde-haired girl slept on, no doubt the effect of the drugs and the other excesses that Sinclair was prone to indulge in... Cathy, or whatever her name was, was merely one in a long line of very young persons that were supplied by the somewhat sordid escort agency that Sinclair patronized.

Clamping a video headset on, Sinclair opened the comm. link and opened the channel. It was the German again. "No, not another infiltration!" The words escaped his mouth involuntarily. The girl stirred but slept on. The details were almost the same as those in the Turkish incident; this time five persons were scanned, but only four were found when the border patrol caught up with them. All four died 'resisting arrest'.

"Wolf," Sinclair peevishly asked, "Does it occur to you that it might be helpful if we could interrogate the infiltrators, and maybe we might learn something," he added sarcastically, "even if it is just one?" Wolf muttered his excuse and abruptly terminated the call.

"Well, this will also have to go to Jim Stewart, I suppose," Sinclair said, "and right away!" So saying, he forwarded a copy of the conversation and Wolf Braun's data file off to John Sanford and Jim Stewart. "Enjoy your day off, Jim!" he muttered. Sinclair returned to the bed, but sleep eluded him so he woke the girl. Soon she was screaming again.

In Euro Central, the heart of the Euro Zone, in the city formerly known as Berlin, Wolf Braun was also having a bad night, but for different reasons. He pored over the intelligence reports from Sanford and the Russian Border patrol. Wolf knew the quality of his personally trained men; they just didn't make mistakes of this sort. Maybe the Turks did, but not his Germans!

Wolf was known for his clinically perfect operations; he was also known for his ruthless intolerance of failure. Wolf had begun his career as an assassin for the Euro Security Agency; he had left many widows in the Russian Federation. His men feared him and made sure that no mistakes were made, ever! Eventually, his leadership qualities had been recognized and he was promoted up the chain, until he now held the top operations position of Deputy Director, in the Euro Security Agency; however, Wolf was ambitious and he coveted that next promotion.

This latest incident therefore, Wolf took very seriously. That someone could evade *his* patrol? Unimaginable! He understood that Dr Jim Stewart might be coming over to look into it, but this was personal to Wolf now! Stewart's reputation as a tracker was legendary; his technical expertise was unequalled too. Why, they all used scanners that Stewart had designed! No, he couldn't allow

Stewart to reveal his failure; and think about the kudos that would accrue for beating the Englishman to the punch!

Wolf reached for the comm. link. Within minutes his crack teams of trackers were on their way to the last sighting point of the infiltration, armed with every available gadget, even dogs, to locate the missing intruder.

Yuri Galenko, leader of the Russian Federation's Trade Commission arrived in Euro Central on the new jetliner that the Europeans had kindly sent to Moscow for his convenience. It was a measure of the importance placed upon the talks that both parties were pulling out all of the stops to make sure that they succeeded. And yet, he had just heard some interesting intercepts coming from the agents in Istanbul... some flap was on. The Euros were scrambling to find some new weapon, it seemed, that the E.A.R. had very carelessly mislaid? Such affairs were not strictly under Yuri's purview, but who knows? Perhaps he could get an edge? Which was all Yuri ever needed. Yes, he would get involved! Even as the plane hovered at the designated landing point Yuri fired off some signals of his own to their Istanbul field office... yes, he would get that edge!

Chen Li, of the E.A.R. Vigilance Directorate scrutinized some reports of his own. They concerned the whereabouts of the traitorous Japanese families, in particular the Hokaida family who had been the prime researchers in the genetics laboratory in Kyoto. The papers which were now untidily stored in boxes around Chen Li's office had all been recovered from that bungled raid on Toshio Hokaida's residence; that had not been done in the right way, as Li had advised his superior officer, General Chi, how it ought to be done. No, Li would have quietly apprehended Hokaida as he walked in the street or when he went to buy vegetables; that was the best way, nice and quietly!

Instead, they rammed the street door, finding it to have been reinforced, and by the time that they had gained control of the situation, Hokaida was dead and his wife and daughter had fled by a prepared escape tunnel. Such a disgrace, but thankfully the accounting was to be the General's, a fact that Chen Li relished.

Li's technical team had recovered some lab samples but they amounted to little more than some green fluid in a refrigerated safe and some inconsequential diaries and mundane laboratory records that were lying around in plain view. The techies were somewhat excited by the fluid, saying that it seemed to be 'new,' but what it was for or how it was used, they were unable to say because a self-destruct mechanism built into the safe had been triggered when the door was forced, leading to the incineration of a number of ledgers and what seemed to have been laboratory experimental records. Again, Li gloated over the scale of General Chi's failure. Such incidents could only be to his advantage when the inevitable fall from favour came for General Chi.

Some references to a related family that had apparently participated in some sort of clinical trial were also found, but that too proved to be a dead end, so far at least, since the two cousins also disappeared immediately after the Hokaida raid. Probably they had all gone underground and would re-emerge later when they judged that the heat was off. Chen Li decided that it would best serve his interests to strongly hint in his report that the Hokaidas had been involved in domestic terrorism and the quantities of green fluid which had been recovered were *most likely* viral agents that would be used in germ warfare against the E.A.R. government. "Yes, that would do nicely," Li concluded, "just enough to muddy the waters, and alert the Central Committee to the incompetence of General Chi!"

He also, as a matter of routine, sent out a general alert to every border security department, circulating a full description of the fugitives, with a specific instruction that they were to be taken alive and returned only to Chen Li for personal interrogation.

Within an hour, over a thousand border crossing posts received the notice. Most just filed it under 'pending' and a few pinned it up next to the border guard officer's desk. Chen Li was a realist; he didn't expect immediate results, but sometimes things did just drop into your hand if you waited patiently!

In just such a way, an hour later, he happened to be passing by the Foreign Affairs Desk in the Ministry as two reports came in from E.A.R. moles

41

in the Euro Zone security offices in London Metropolis and Euro Central. The moles reported that the Euros were flapping over some infiltrators that had dropped out of sight; what *was* interesting was that the signal traffic had been going on at the highest level.

Chen Li was definitely interested now. "What was so special about these infiltrators?" Then in a flash of sheer brilliance, he intuitively realized that this was somehow connected with the export of germ warfare materials to Euro Zone by his fugitives. He immediately sent out another alert, raised the alert status to 'Top Urgent', and then he called his boss.

General Chi was understandably furious that his bungling was now a matter of public record and the fugitives were now deemed to be vital to the security of the E.A.R. In order to show that he was on top of the situation, he therefore initiated a call to the Ministry for Foreign Affairs and spoke to the Minister, briefing him about the emergency.

The next action came quickly. All foreign active and sleeper agents were contacted and ordered to locate and eliminate the threat; all internal security forces were also placed on emergency alert status and prepared for mobilization. The hunt was on!

Chapter Four: A Haven of Rest

The Exeter Express arrived at Castle Cary Station somewhat later than the timetable had promised. It was a small station serving Middle Somerset, and it was used mainly by commuters to London Metropolis who wished to take advantage of the clean fresh country air and didn't object to the one hour journey by the high speed express trains that served the West Country every hour. Castle Cary was a very old station, and still had only three platforms – two for the local traffic – but at this early hour it was completely deserted except for the robotic cleaning machines that scoured the platforms and maglev tracks looking for litter.

Since the train had already been searched and cleared at Andover, the local Defenders Office didn't even bother to glance out of the window of their warm and comfortable checkpoint, so the trio who dismounted the train passed by unseen.

On the helipad, the farm's rotor vehicle waited patiently for their arrival. The automatic pilot greeted Dr Jim as he placed his hand on the door ID pad. "Hello, Dr Jim Stewart, I have been programmed to fly you to the farm at Priddy. Are there any changes to the flight plan?"

"No," replied Jim, "take us up carefully please as we have new passengers on board."

"Yes, of course sir! I wish to remind you that I have an excellent skill rating and nil accidents on my record," the machine responded. Jim sighed; sometimes this Artificial Intelligence was just too much! "OK, let's skip the chatter. Take us home if you please."

The rotor vehicle slowly and silently lifted off from the helipad, the modified helicopter blades making barely a whisper on the morning air, unheard by the Defenders on duty at the station only fifty metres away. Dawn was breaking as they rose above the treetops and the rotor vehicle moved quickly across the open fields at low altitude until it had cleared the area of Castle Cary. Then, gaining altitude, it silently moved northwest towards Priddy. Beneath them, the roads and lanes were deserted of traffic. For the most part this countryside would have looked the same for the past two hundred years, with the exception of the robotic farming machines that tilled and cultivated the chalky soils of the valley throughout the day and night, using their solar panels to charge the fuel cells that powered them.

"This is farming country," Jim informed Sakura. "I bought a farm here from the royalties I earn from my devices. My brothers Bill and John live out here too. We do keep a few sheep and cows, mostly for appearances' sake; we like to see them graze out in the fields. It's more organic I guess too. But mostly, we develop our new scanners and suchlike in the lab on the farm and then we send them for manufacture in mainland Euro Zone, in Dusseldorf actually, where we have an affiliate company. In any case, I'm away quite a lot on Government business. It's very private on the farm, no visitors usually, so you will be very secure there."

Sakura and Grace looked excitedly out of the window for the whole flight. Every grazing animal gave occasion for more excited giggles from Grace; it was as if she had never seen cows and sheep before. Jim glanced over from time to time and one time his eyes met Sakura's. Her amazing eyes flashed and she smiled at him, truly happy and contented to be heading to her new home.

"Just wait," Jim smiled back, "I've got a special surprise for you when we land!"

"Do tell me please!" she entreated.

"Nope, you've just to see it, no good telling you about this! And you, young Grace, stop scanning me; you'll spoil the surprise for Mummy!"

It was dawn as they made the final approach to the farm, a huddle of three cottages built in the traditional local style using local stone and tile roofs. The farm lay outside the village and seemed to cling to the limestone bluff at the end of a broad valley. Small farms dotted the Priddy landscape and sheep grazed in the fields which were bounded by dry stone walls built of the local stone in an ages-old traditional skill and in the lower land there were dense hedgerows. The stone walls glowed gold in the first rays of the sunrise which broke over the Mendip Hills about the farm.

"This is a very ancient area," Jim informed Sakura. "This whole area is a honeycomb of old mine workings, they used to mine for copper and tin around these parts; and because this is a mainly limestone area, there are many existing cave systems too. The mine tunnels often broke through into the natural passageways as they were being worked. This makes it an ideal location for those who wish to establish some privacy in their comings and goings and incidentally, because most of these old workings have never been mapped, we can set up routes for escape that can never be traced! Perhaps one of these days I'll show you the local sights; there is a site of a Roman encampment and a Roman Road used to run nearby the farm; there are also some prehistoric remains that are perhaps a little more interesting. There is a group of twenty ancient burial mounds which are called tumuli or barrows; we call them the Priddy Barrows. These date back to the late Neolithic period. Then nearby, there are ten Bronze Age round barrows; and not far off are the Priddy Circles, as they are called; this is a complex with three circles of large standing posts; it's been restored and quite huge actually, something like the more famous monument of Stonehenge. There are some people who believe that these ancient circles harness special psychic power and these ancient monuments are linked with what they call ley-lines. All absolute rubbish, in my humble opinion, no one has ever established the presence of such lines by any scientific enquiry!"

"OK, now it's time to close your eyes. It's time for your first surprise!"

Sakura and Grace dutifully closed their eyes tightly as the rotor vehicle touched down gently at the far end of the farm's driveway. Jim carefully helped them to dismount and led them to the centre of the driveway. "OK, you can open your eyes now," Jim whispered.

Immediately, there were two sharp intakes of breath. "Jim, oh, this is wonderful!" Sakura exclaimed. "You've planted a whole driveway of cherry trees, Japanese Cherry Trees! How wonderful, what a beautiful surprise for us. Look Grace, it's just like home!"

The trees stretched out in a double row either side of the driveway until the cottages, their branches already bearing the buds that would soon blossom and create the breathtaking vista of pink and white that comes every spring in Kyoto.

"Jim, why did you do this?" she asked breathlessly.

"Well, it was to remind me of my friend, Toshio. I hoped that one day he would come to see me when the cherry blossoms bloomed. I never dreamt that it would be his daughter and granddaughter that would actually come!"

"I am sure that you never knew that you really planted these trees for me, for actually this is the meaning of my name… Sakura means 'Cherry Blossom'! Perhaps this is fate," she concluded softly, "I am meant to be here!"

They walked along the avenue of trees and there to meet them at the end of the walk were his brothers, Bill and Jim, who greeted the new arrivals in their usual boisterous way. The three brothers bore a strong resemblance, tall and handsome in a rugged sort of way. Each of them

47

had served in the UK Army, Bill as an Engineering Officer and John as a Sapper. Young Grace squealed with delight as she was hoisted up onto her Uncle John's shoulders and they trotted off to the cottage that belonged to Jim. Sakura was also greeted with their customary friendliness, a handshake followed by a hug, a little to her discomfort.

"Any problems on the way, pal?" asked Bill.

"Well, yes and no! I think we'd better go inside and I'll tell you all about it. This is a two cuppa tea type of story!" added Jim.

First of all, they showed Sakura and Grace around the cottage. A small bed was already made up for Grace and sheepishly they admitted that they were not sure what the other sleeping arrangement was going to be, so Sakura's bed was not made.

"That's fine," said Jim, "she and Grace will share a room for now, but maybe later there will be some changes." Sakura blushed a deep shade of red upon hearing this. "Look, I know this is rushing things a bit, Sakura, but the kid has to have a legal father you know!"

"Oh, yes, I understand what you mean now." She sighed, "Everything has to be legalized so we can stay in England. But what we shall we do for the others, Asuka and Ren, when they arrive here?"

"They are coming here too?" Jim asked, totally surprised by this latest revelation. "You never happened to mention that little detail in our conversation on the Maglev train!"

48

"It's got to be," Sakura stated flatly, "it's the only way!"

"Hmm, I guess so, I just never thought about it..." Jim's voiced trailed off.

"Well, if you girls are all so damn gorgeous, I don't think you'll have to look too far for spouses for your friends!" interjected John, with a twinkle in his eye.

"Well, they are my cousins, actually, and you will have to judge for yourself, John," she replied, with a smile. "I may be biased, but I think that they are indeed 'gorgeous' as you put it!"

Everyone laughed at that and the tour was seemingly over, until Grace, started saying, "Mummy, down, Mummy down!"

Sakura looked blank, but then Jim cut in, "I guess it's impossible to keep a secret from a telepath!"

He walked over to the door of the bedroom explaining, "If you stand exactly here and touch this hidden panel in the wall here, you will see what Grace has discovered." A whole section of the floor slid smoothly back, revealing steps that led down. Following the steps, they came into a huge cavern, which was a workshop and a laboratory used for Jim's special projects.

Jim explained, "When we bought the farm we had to do some relaying of the old flooring. We found a fissure in the bedrock of the floor and accidentally broke through into this place. It's what is called a swallow hole; you can find them in limestone areas above old tunnels. Don't worry, it's perfectly safe. The walls of the swallow hole make a natural arch to the ceiling and give structural support. I dare say you could drive a heavy tank over that floor and it would bear the weight easily. Now, over here is the tunnel that connects us to Bill and John's cottages; they also have a similar access to the tunnel system from their quarters. And over here is my pride and joy! Down the old tunnel-way, we have constructed an escape route. See the three capsules standing along the wall? They are big enough for two persons each, at a pinch. You just stand inside and press that lever down and the capsule will shoot down, propelled by compressed air, finally reaching the end of the tube at the tunnel's end, which is about a kilometre away!"

"But, Jim!" Sakura exclaimed, "This must have cost a fortune, and how long did it all take... years?"

"Well, actually no," Jim replied. "As to the finances, that was no problem for me. I am very wealthy now, every scanner you see in the airports etcetera is a Stewart Scanner, many of them made under license, even in the E.A.R., and I get a royalty fee on every scanner that you see because my scanners are better than my competitors. As for the construction work, I have to give most of the credit for that to my brothers; Bill is a whiz with the robotics, he both built the robots that developed the tunnel and enclosed it with a welded steel tube; John built the control systems and the capsules; and some of the other security features all around the farm buildings were my handiwork."

"OK folks, I guess that is enough for now. Let's go eat!"

On the hills above the Stewart Farm, a lone watcher lay unseen in the coarse pasture margin, his body clad in a green suit. No thermal image would have been seen, and the suit afforded him a perfect camouflage as it automatically blended to the natural colours of the ground where he lay. The watcher had been in position on the hillside for the past twenty-four hours, only moving under cover of darkness for a call of nature. Every hour, he would send a high frequency burst transmission that lasted a mere five seconds, undetectable unless you were expecting it. The transmission was expected and the report was duly noted in the operations log.

The farmhouse warmed to the smell of cooking and coffee brewing. Easy conversation was shared around the table as the enlarged family sat down to eat. "Now this is a proper English breakfast, young John," Jim exclaimed, "boy did you learn something useful while you were in the Army! I could have killed for some of this when I was in India, absolutely nothing decent to eat there anymore!" They all sat in silence for a while, reflecting upon the awful events that had scarred that beautiful land, even up into the high Himalayas where Jim had been. "Pakistan, they say it is even worse, the Hindu Kush is still blackened and it may be years before the radiation levels will allow recolonisation of the high country. The water flowing down from the Himalayas is all contaminated still; God knows how it's affecting their populations; probably lots of birth defects and cancers, I shouldn't wonder! I don't know how long it will take to reach safe levels of radiation again!" They all sat quietly considering the futility of war.

Then eventually Bill spoke up, "By the way, Jim, on your travels did you ever see one of these before?" he handed a small badge to Jim, "what do you make of this?" The badge was in the form of a pair of angel's wings.

"Where did you find this, Bill?" Jim asked sharply.

"Why, it was lying on my doorstep, I found it when I went out to send the rotor vehicle down to pick you up."

"Umm," Jim pondered this for a while, then he smiled as he announced to the table, "Lady and gentlemen, we have angels watching over us! This is the badge, the emblem, of the Resistance movement known as The Angels. This is a message to give us hope!"

"Sakura, did you tell anyone that we were coming here? Who else knows about your trip to England?"

She replied, "Jim, all of our ID's and journey were arranged by the Underground in Japan, they have international links all over Europe, and throughout the world in fact. They are cooperating with many national groups for this mission, for that is what this is, a most important mission that will bring about a radically new world!"

"Wow!" said John, "and there I was thinking that you were just a couple of backpackers that Jim had picked up!"

Jim decided that this was the time to fill his brothers in on the whole story. As he related the history of Toshio and Glenda in Korea, the flight to Japan and ultimately Sakura's arrival in Priddy, they sat enrapt; the coffee grew cold on the table.

Chapter Five: Ministering Angels

Asuka and Akiyoshi, the boy child, sat huddled under an awning and several insulated blankets on the barge which was moving north on the River Rhine. Its cargo was manufactured goods from Cologne bound for Amsterdam. From time to time, patrol boats of the German Defenders Brigade passed by. It was all routine, but to be on the safe side the barge operator had placed lead sheets around the hiding place; enough for a routine surface scan, but not for an aerial heat sensor imaging scan or a boarding party. They would just have to pray that the supervisor of the German hunter teams, who happened to be Wolf Braun, would not decide to increase the level of surveillance to include thermal imaging!

So far their luck had been incredibly good; they had crossed the Czech border between Prague and Dresden; the first time Akiyoshi had to use his telepathy was to confuse some Czech border guards with dogs who almost stumbled upon them. The dogs had run off howling and in the ensuing confusion, the couple had slipped away silently. They then flagged down a ground car travelling north and the elderly German couple was so taken with the small boy who chattered incessantly with them in perfect German, that they shared their coffee and sausages with the hungry duo; afterwards, Asuka and Akiyoshi slept all the way to the city of Dresden.

There they passed easily through the main Rail Station gate and its scanners and boarded the Leipzig Intercity Maglev train without further incident because the boy used his telepathic skills with the ticket collector. The man happily issued them a First Class through ticket all the way to Koblenz. Naturally, being in the carriages normally only used by the elite members of the ruling party, they were warm and comfortable and left undisturbed throughout the night; so they were able to make up for some lost sleep.

The Underground had arranged for transit visas for Asuka and Akiyoshi, whose name means 'bright and good', and everything so far was going according to his name for them, exactly following the plan which had been meticulously drawn up in Japan. They decided that they would use the legal documents that they carried only when they reached Amsterdam, where document examination of transiting visitors was likely to be more stringent.

The operator of the barge had been handsomely compensated for his assistance but there was always a remote possibility that the barge deckhands might engage in loose talk later, so the two passengers kept a silent vigil, sustained by coffee and sandwiches which were supplied by the barge operator when they boarded. To all intents and purposes, they were like ghosts in the night.

The barge kept up a slow but steady pace; its arrival in Amsterdam was due at nightfall, then they would be taken in hand by the local Dutch Underground. The plan was for the Underground's agent to get them onto a fast boat to Essex, in South East England, where the planned landfall was Tollesbury in the Essex marshes. Their landing point had been chosen carefully. That part of the coastline had a history of cross channel trade under cover of darkness and people who lived around the area tended to mind their own business when they heard sounds in the marshes at night.

The marshes, which were navigable for only two hours at high tide, offered the type of seclusion that they were looking for; because of the numerous inlets it was impossible for the Defenders or Customs agents to mount effective patrolling within the marshes. For this same reason, generations of smugglers before them had used this route to bring fine French brandy and other dutiable or contraband goods across these salt marshes for the tables of the nobility in London, which was only seventy kilometres from Tollesbury Village.

The passage through Amsterdam had gone surprisingly smoothly; their documents raised no alarms and they indicated to the transit police that they would be travelling south to Utrecht and in fact rail seats were purchased in their names; but the actual travellers were a couple of students who were told that they had won a spot prize awarded by Netherlands Rail Authority. If the hunters were successful in tracking them to Amsterdam, the Underground hoped that this ruse would buy them enough time to complete the transfer to England. But just to make certain that the Dutch Defenders Force had plenty to occupy their minds away from

Amsterdam; some small explosions were organized at Eindhoven and Arnhem in the Railway Stations' left luggage storage rooms. Nothing like sowing confusion!

Money lubricates the way in most ports of the world and Amsterdam was no exception, if you knew the right person to approach. Here it secured for Asuka and Akiyoshi a fast skimmer boat, powered by a T-drive marine engine, and this low profile boat was capable of 60 knots in open water. Being almost invisible to radar and very fast it was the ideal vessel for their crossing, but the ride was horrendously rough once they reached the mid-Channel waves, so that it wasn't long before the coffee and sandwiches that they had consumed in Amsterdam re-emerged and disappeared over the side.

The pilot never spoke once throughout the entire crossing, which suited them just fine. By the time that they made landfall in Tollesbury they were soaked with spray and feeling very sick and bruised indeed. There was very poor visibility owing to a dense fog over the coast; the moon was on the wane; everything seemed perfect, but as the skimmer's Captain slowed their engine to a crawling speed, they heard the deep booming of the Customs Patrol boat. The Captain cut the engine and motioning for absolute silence, he let the boat drift under the overhanging reeds at the edge of the mouth of a small channel. The sound of the Customs Patrol boat's engine grew nearer; its marine engines gave a deep and powerful beat on the night air. A powerful searchlight played over the tops of the reed beds and along every tributary channel. They sat silently; there was only the lapping of the tidal stream on the hull of the skimmer. Every metallic surface on their craft was painted over black, so there would be no reflection of a searchlight's beam. The reeds fell over their boat like a curtain and the fog was their friend as the searchlight could not penetrate more than fifteen metres through the swirling mist. The patrol boat passed them by, only twenty metres away, but they were safe! The sound of the motor slowly faded, and after waiting a few minutes more to be sure that the Customs Patrol would not be returning, the Captain restarted the skimmer's engine in whisper mode; no sense in taking any chances tonight.

To Asuka and Akiyoshi the reed beds seemed a solid wall of vegetation, but the Captain seemed to sense rather than see the inlet channel that he needed. The skimmer edged slowly deeper into the marshes, still no navigation lights showing, the powerful engine making only a gentle purr as the boat moved carefully along the silted waterway which led deep into the marsh.

After perhaps fifteen minutes, they moored at an ancient looking jetty; the Captain flashed his light in the prearranged signal sequence and then they waited. The minutes dragged by and nothing stirred in the darkness around them; had something gone wrong?

Then a signal; a red light flashed out at them three times from the land and at the Captain's urgent gesture, they jumped ashore. Immediately the skimmer's Captain released the mooring rope and slowly backed out into the main channel and then headed just as carefully back out to the sea. Fifteen or so minutes later the roar of its T-drive could be heard pulsating out on the open sea and they were left to the silence of the marshes, and the gathering fog. The night air was punctuated by the screeching calls of the occasional lonely seagull which circled in the fog above them.

Presently, the sounds of sea boots on the planking of the jetty informed them of the arrival of their hosts. There was only one person to meet them. "Shh!" the man's gruff voice said, "sounds travel far over water, you know. I am Andrew, welcome to England. Come, let's go quickly before the Defenders come sniffing around here!"

They quickly filed along the jetty until they reached a path which ran along the edge of a salt bund. They skirted the houses of Tollesbury Village, which stood above the tidal waters on stilts, looking for all the world like some alien life forms that might stride off into the mists; strange creatures of the night.

After the trio had walked a while, Akiyoshi asked to be carried, as he was tired. Andrew immediately scooped him up, all the while urging them on faster. When they reached the lane, after a further ten minutes brisk walking on the slippery paths, they came to his ground car, which lay concealed behind some scrub bush, totally invisible to a passing patrol. They crouched behind the vehicle while Andrew made a quick radio call to someone. In the distance and inland, there was a loud explosion, followed by what sounded like small arms fire. The radio squawked again and then fell silent. "Don't worry," said Andrew, "the Defenders patrol just hit a landmine and my friends took out the crew too. We should go now, and quickly, before someone else comes looking."

The ground car started silently, being electric. Its fuel cell was fully charged, with more than enough power for the seventy-two kilometre run to London Metropolis.

"Ever use one of these?" asked Andrew, passing her a short-range laser pistol. "They're accurate enough for close work, just in case there are any roadblocks. The Angels are running interference for us anyway. When we reach Maldon we shall avoid New London proper and take the old Circular Route around the new North London Super Dome, then, after reaching the suburb of Watford, we shall set off west across country until we reach your destination. The range of my vehicle is about two hundred and fifty kilometres but on the back roads we shall not get that range, so we shall change vehicles along the way, kinda like a relay!"

"It's going to be a rather long journey, I'm afraid, so I suggest that you try to get some rest. I'll alert you if there are any roadblocks or check points ahead."

Asuka agreed, then added, "Give me plenty of warning of the checkpoints, I can handle that situation."

Andrew looked at her quizzically. "I wonder what she meant by that? Must have banged her head pretty hard on that sea crossing, shouldn't wonder!"

The third child, a girl named Akemi, and her mother Ren were stuck in Istanbul. Things hadn't gone as smoothly there for Akemi as for the other two children. Partly this was because a Japanese woman stuck out like a sore thumb in Istanbul and being accompanied by a Eurasian minor just added to the difficulty of navigating around the city. The Angels had provided them shelter in a slum quarter, which they believed would be safer than staying in the new districts of the city.

The house was old, overcrowded and crumbling. The haze of smoke from wood-fired stoves lit inside the tenants' rooms ensured that the hordes of biting insects were kept at bay, but the down side was that the smell of fire clung to their garments in spite of Ren's attempt to ventilate their room with an open window. From time to time, one of the Angels would stop by to bring them fresh water and food, which despite the filthy outsides of the containers, was clean and delicious. Sleep was elusive because of the incessant din of the neighbourhood; children wailed, dogs barked, donkeys brayed and Turkish music was played loudly throughout the night.

A Lebanese gentleman, whose name was given as Gabriel, had approached the Angels' agents who were watching over them; quite how he located them in the sprawling slum where they were hidden was quite a feat in itself. He eventually managed to gain access to Ren by quoting the name of Dr Jim Stewart, Akemi's father. He said that Dr Stewart had sent word to him through his representative in Istanbul and Gabriel had agreed to look into it. The only negative news was that in the course of his discreet enquiries, he had discovered that a veritable pack of agents was also hunting for the couple; E.A.R., Russians and Germans, and they were splashing money around like champagne at a wedding to get a lead on them. It was clearly going to be tricky to get them out of the city, and dangerous for them to stay put in this house any longer.

Gabriel didn't know how far ahead of the pack he was, but it stood to reason that the hunters were eventually going to strike pay dirt and couldn't be far behind him! Gabriel, however, had a plan. He had tried to put himself in the minds of the hunters; what would they expect the 'infiltrators' to do? Flee, obviously, but which way; by sea or land, west, north or south?

Gabriel decided that they would opt for the O-3 Highway going west from Istanbul. Crossing the border into Bulgaria would be simple since they were already in the Euro Zone. Yes, they would expect an overland car journey or possibly public transport via Bulgaria; then there was a choice to go via Albania or Greece! He examined his road maps to see which less obvious route they could take.

Gabriel was confident that there would be an opportunity to use either Sabika Gokcen Havaalani

International Airport, which was near to Atabey on the southern coast; or even sixty-eight kilometres north east of that airport, there was Cengiz Topel Naval Air Station, an airfield at Kocaali, which was in joint use by the military and civilian users. A small jet landing there would not draw undue attention.

He decided that their best option was to leave Istanbul under cover of darkness that night and travel down the D100 highway through Gebze until Izmit and then follow the O-4 superhighway heading eastward and rejoin the D100 until Hendek; then they would turn north along the minor road to Kocaali passing through Kahraman. Although Cengiz Topel was further away, Gabriel felt instinctively that the smaller airport would offer more opportunity to make a deal with the guards on duty at the airport gate.

Yes, he would tell Ahmet that this was where Dr Jim could collect the mother and child. Perhaps some palms would have to be greased, but this was normal business. Of course, there was the possibility that one of the hunter teams might think along the same line as Gabriel, but then, if so, Sabika Gokeen would be the first place for them to look, and that would give him even more time to elude the chase. The road up to Kocaali from Hendek was a mountain road, so their speed would be restricted and there was the chance of being seen from below as they navigated the pass. He had to count upon getting a head start and boldness for success! It was a risky plan, but there was no time to look for another. They had best leave as soon as possible, in fact tonight!

Gabriel made contact with Dr Jim's representative, Ahmet, and explained the change of plan. Ahmet agreed and said that he would make contact immediately with Dr Jim by encrypted signal to Jim's home network, which was as secure a transmission as it was possible to make. Ahmet also promised Gabriel that his loyalty would be rewarded with a healthy bonus upon delivery of the couple to him at Kocaali. Gabriel rubbed his hands joyfully. "Now, everyone we have to be busy, so let's be busy!"

Within the hour, a car left the gate of the building which was in the slum area of Salacak. This was no polished electric car powered by a fuel cell like the one presently carrying the other child to the West of England; it was a very ancient diesel-engine Mercedes, a veritable museum piece. It had to be fifty years old! But Turkey was a backwater of the Euro Zone and only in the cities would there be electric cars on the roads. In the provinces, an old diesel car would fit right in; no one would pay attention to it. The last thing that Gabriel wanted to do was to stand out, or be memorable for those that the hunters would interrogate later.

Even at this late hour, the streets of Salacak were busy, cars honked and donkeys brayed in protest as their owners fought for advantage in the traffic jammed streets of the old city. Progress was necessarily slow at first but once they reached the outskirts of the old quarter, they picked up speed and joined the exodus onto D100. Gabriel kept up a steady banter with the girl, Akemi, who he was amazed to discover was able to discourse with him perfectly in both Turkish and Arabic. He tried out some French with her, and when she replied also in perfect French, with a Lebanese accent, he decided to quit while he was ahead.

In spite of the Mercedes' age, it made very good time on the main road, and within two hours they had reached Gebze. The next sector to Izmit took only an hour as the traffic by now was very light on the O-4 superhighway. Before they reached Hendek junction and immediately after rounding a sharp bend, Gabriel suddenly switched off the lights and swerved off the road. He expertly slipped the car behind some trees and then waited.

Two minutes later, an electric ground car swished past their hiding place. Unseen themselves but able to see the road clearly in the moonlight, they saw the faces of the Chinese occupants of the pursuing ground car as they strained forward, looking down the road to Hendek.

"How did you know, Gabriel?" Ren asked him.

"Sometimes, I don't know how, but the hairs on the back of my neck just sort of tingle," he replied. "Whenever I have obeyed that as a warning, I have been alright, so I just keep doing it!" Then he added, "So what do we do now? They may decide to double back any minute when they don't find us down the road."

"Well, we have a secret weapon that they don't know about!" she replied.

A few minutes later, sure enough, the Chinese returned, now searching the road margins with a powerful flashlight mounted on the roof of the ground car. They drove quite slowly so that they couldn't fail to see the Mercedes in the shadows under the trees. Gabriel cocked his pistol, ready to go down blazing.

"No need, Uncle," Akemi said to him in Arabic and, to Gabriel's utter amazement, the other vehicle just continued on past them; the eyes of the Chinese E.A.R. agents looked straight at them, but didn't see them; it was as if they were invisible!

"Amazing, that's absolutely amazing!" Gabriel announced and they all laughed heartily. The crisis was over and they could relax

From that point on they continued to make good time and there were no more scares. They had passed the turning for Sabika Gokcen Havaalani International Airport much earlier and it was very busy with tourist flights coming and going. For a moment Gabriel wondered whether he had made the right choice; perhaps they could have hidden in the crowds which would throng the Departures Hall? No, on reflection, when he considered the calibre of these hunters, that choice was doubtful of success. The E.A.R. agents were supposed to be the best in the business at what they did; a crowded hall would not stop them!

They pressed on, pushing the old Mercedes to its limit. The road grew quiet again, now it was just them and the night. The road twisted and turned through the West Anatolian countryside, heading up into the high mountain ranges as they left the fertile plains below them. If they had been in the daylight, the view would have been of mile upon mile of fruit trees; apricot, fig and plums, all in early Spring bloom.

The road continued to climb, the Mercedes' tyres squealing on the hairpin bends as Gabriel struggled to master the heavy old car up the mountain road.

Eventually they were within sight of Cengiz Topel Airport and Gabriel announced that it would be better for him to go on alone to negotiate for their entry into the restricted area. To his great surprise, Ren and Akemi disagreed.

Ren told him, "Let us come along, you have seen what Akemi is capable of doing already. If she wanted, she could have the guard making tea for us while we wait for Dr Stewart!"

"Yes, I'll just bet that she could, she could indeed," agreed Gabriel, nodding his head.

As the trio prepared to enter the airfield, at Hendek, the Russian team of four hunters had stumbled across the returning Chinese agents. It was clear to the Russians that the E.A.R. team must be on the same mission because it was so unusual to see Chinese so far from the cities and in the early hours of the morning.

They pulled over to discuss the implications of a hunter team heading west; had they found their quarry, or perhaps they had given up on the chase? The reputation of the E.A.R. killer squads convinced them that the second choice was most unlikely; they argued the pros and cons of ending the chase.

In the end it was the team leader who made the decision. "Look, we don't know anything yet for certain, *maybe* the Chinese have terminated the woman and the girl, but we don't know that for sure. We have come so far already; it would be crazy to turn back unless we are sure that the quarries are dead. Sabika Gokcen Havaalani Airport is a few kilometres back up the road; that is where they are heading for sure. We will go and check out the road that leads to the airport or if we find the car on the roadside we will know that it is over." They all agreed; he was, in any case, the nephew of Yuri Galenko, and to disagree might be seriously prejudicial to their careers. Also, they all agreed that since this was after all only a fishing expedition that Yuri Galenko had requested… not a prime directive. They would abort the mission if they had reasonable evidence that it was right to do so. They would then inform Yuri that the Chinese had eliminated their objective and they saw no point in exposing their presence in the country to some provincial cop who might wonder what they were doing hanging around airfields in the early hours of the morning.

Unfortunately, they were just as conspicuous to the Chinese team on that deserted highway. The

E.A.R. car pulled over onto the side shoulder. They immediately went through a similar discussion to the Russians. Surely those were agents also? Maybe they have a solid lead on the Japanese woman and the young girl? To have another hunter team take their prize away from them would be a terrible loss of face for General Chi, one person that you'd never want to get on the wrong side of! The E.A.R squad raced along the road to Sabika Gokcen Havaalani Airport. They would forgo sleep a while longer.

Gabriel, Ren and Akemi were inside the airfield. As it turned out, the guard was inattentive to his duty; the gates were unlocked and he had decided to answer a call of nature. While he was busy with his toilet, the trio simply hid the Mercedes and then walked past silently on the grass verge; he never knew that they had been there. Akemi sent him an urgent reminder to lock the gates, which he did whilst fumbling with his trousers. Now if anyone else came along, they'd have to talk to the guard before he would admit them.

They headed for a row of four civilian hangars, which were closest to the runway. The sheds were deserted and in total darkness; perfect for their purposes! They checked out the first hangar but it was completely bare, no place to hide there! Then they entered the second hangar in the row and looked around for somewhere warm to wait where there was a view of the apron and the runway. A heap of tarpaulin covers lay carelessly heaped in a corner; that would be ideal for their purposes!

There was only one runway, and it was not very long, but in these days of VTOL no one built long runways anymore. Occasionally a Turkish Air Force or Naval Patrol plane would land and then taxi off to the other side of the field, where all of the military installations were grouped. The hours ticked by slowly.

Gabriel decided to risk a call to Ahmet. "Any word yet?"

"No," Ahmet replied, "still trying to confirm that Jim is on the way. What's your situation?"

"Well," Gabriel replied, "Some Chinese agents came very close to us, but I think we gave them the slip for now. Don't know about the Germans or the Russians though!"

"Forget the German squad, my team planted some false leads; last seen they were heading for the Fatherland, by way of Bulgaria, Greece and the Balkans!" They both chuckled at that one. "Seriously now, Gabriel, keep your head down, these guys looking for you three are really bad people!;

"OK will do. Let me know when you have an E.T.A. for Dr Jim."

Ahmet turned to his comms link and fired off a second round of code. This time he included an alarm tone in the send instruction. Jim would definitely respond quickly now.

Chapter Six: An Early Call

Ahmet's first message had been received by Jim already but he was now trying to negotiate a plane for his urgent need. Then he remembered that he had promised Sinclair that he would personally go to Turkey to investigate the infiltration... why not put it on the Progress Party's bill?

Just as Ahmet's second call came in, Jim had concluded his negotiation for a plane. The best airfield for Jim's purposes was Yeovilton, in Somerset, which was not too far from Priddy, if he took the rotor vehicle. Yeovilton happened to be Euro Zone's busiest military airfield and it served as a home base to the Naval Helicopter Squadron and the elite Commando Forces. Generally there were three thousand military and civilian personnel on the base at any one time, so Jim's comings and goings would not really occasion much comment; it would be thought that his was another of those covert ops that the military usually ran out of Yeovilton. Besides, the Base Commander was an ex-Corps buddy who was always ready to bend the rules for Jim!

Jim fired off a reply to Ahmet. He would fly down to Yeovilton and transfer to a Jump Jet hired by the Government for his mission. Strictly speaking, the jet was a two-seater but quite roomy, so they would manage to squeeze Akemi between them somehow. Jim figured that his ETA would be eight o'clock local time in Kocaali; Ahmet sent his acknowledgement by return.

Owing to his military flying license, Jim was given some leeway by his friend the Base Commander, so he was to fly the plane himself. This made everything much simpler, there would be no talkative pilot to reveal what he had really been up to in Turkey!

The Scranton Jump Jet was the Euro Zone's workhorse fighter. Carrying hefty weaponry, it was useful for medium range missions and close quarters combat. It utilised the latest Artificial Intelligence (AI) for flight control, had good manoeuvrability, and it was decidedly the quickest jet available for Jim without special authorization of the top brass. At Jim's insistence the jet was given a full armament load, you never knew what might come up on these missions! Jim's flight was given priority one clearance by the controller and the autopilot fired up the engines. Hopefully, all Jim would need to do was to sit back and hold on to his breakfast.

The jet lifted off in its customary jerky style but once airborne it clicked smoothly into Jump Mode in seconds. The Scranton flew really fast; it knew where it was going and did that with no-nonsense efficiency. Within three minutes, the jet had jumped to Mach one, and still accelerating continually, it hit fifteen thousand metres altitude two minutes later doing Mach two. Using Sinclair's clout, Jim had obtained an emergency flight plan, which was duly electronically filed with Kocaali. It was going to be a good day and the sun was forecast to be shining all the way!

Chapter Seven: Angels Gathering

The sub-ether link crackled slightly and then the voices came through clearly. The representatives of the Resistance, Underground, Angel network; call it what you will, they alone represented the true voice of the peoples of the world. Resistance to the combined might of totalitarian governments had grown from citywide to national and finally international cooperation.

Their legitimate routes to political representation and justice having being denied, the people first did what they could to register their concerns in peaceful ways; anti-government posters, graffiti, even hijacking Government controlled wavebands to voice their protests. All had been met with brutal repression and these methods had been largely ineffective, if effectiveness can be measured by achieving an end result.

However, a groundswell of righteous protest was growing and an escalation to general armed resistance now seemed more than just inevitable, it was a fact.

The power blocs of Euro Zone, E.A.R., Russian Federation and the emerging Union of American States now experienced guerrilla attacks on a daily basis. The attacks were targeted at government establishments, government controlled media and power infrastructure for maximum visibility and propaganda. The response of the dictatorships and hegemonies to every form of resistance was predictable; more repression, which naturally inspired more resistance. The truth of the matter was that the balance of power lay now with the people; the old regimes were doomed. It was only a matter of time and finding the right catalyst to set off a domino effect. Both of these were now the subject of the sub-ether conference.

Duane Richards, Union of the Americas, acting as the Chairman for the discussion, said, "Do we have a consensus for the strike date?"

The delegates all concurred. "Japan, speaking; yes, we feel that the World Council Conference to be held on May first in London is the best opportunity that we shall have when all of the main leaders will attend. If we do not manage this date then we will have to wait until next year for such a gathering."

"Netherlands speaking; we also believe that the strike must be decisive. Partial success is not enough, because it will result in the survivors changing their security protocols and this will complicate a second attempt."

"Agreed," they all intoned.

Richards interjected, "And what about the assets, are they in place yet?"

Jack Bailey, UK Angels Network replied, "We are still in process of assembling them; one more asset is on the way and then we will be ready. We are maintaining a protective shield about the in-country assets and facilitating the arrival of the last one. We shall be ready before the Council meeting."

"What about the second phase? Do we have the synthetic material ready, and is it effective?"

"Japan here; yes, the answer to both questions is absolutely affirmative, the synthetic is actually more powerful than the original and has a quicker response time!" Everyone cheered at that. Presently, Richards called them to order and closed the meeting with the words; "It's a go then!"

Chapter Eight: Retaliation

John Sanford was once a good cop and an excellent detective. He had risen through the ranks to the position of Assistant Chief Constable in the Merseyside Metropolitan Police, but there his career had stalled. He always felt that he was passed over because he didn't have the requisite airs and graces of the other candidates, who certainly had pedigrees that were more to the liking of the panel of Chief Constables that denied him what he felt was his due. In his heart resentment festered like an open sore that would not heal; one day, he knew, he would take his revenge on those pompous old farts!

Sanford always said that it was the luckiest day of his life that, as he happened to be doing a routine tour of inspection of the Central Police Station cells in Liverpool, he came into contact with a man called Ian McGregor. McGregor was being held on suspicion of involvement in a particularly nasty assault upon a political candidate in the upcoming Merseyside By-Elections. Sanford recognized McGregor; he had heard rumours about McGregor's tactics and the methods of the fledgling Progress Party.

Sanford was somewhat sympathetic to the notion that Britain's ills stemmed from an undermining of the nation's confidence by generations of Asian immigrants and he was well aware of the extent to which the Asian gangs had taken over whole city centres, imposing defacto no-go areas for the Police, where gangs warred continually and drugs and prostitution were everywhere. Sanford despised the weakness of the Coalition Government. They seemed incapable of exerting proper authority. If he had the power, Sanford vowed, he would sweep the vermin off the streets for good, clean the country of these 'pollutants' and brings things back to a proper balance, an orderly society.

McGregor himself was a candidate in this by-election, and it was alleged that he had assaulted the complainant with a club, and slashed his face with a razor. Neither of the weapons was found in the immediate vicinity nor could any witnesses be found to corroborate the charges being made. However, a razor had been found in an alley nearby and it was submitted to Forensics for examination.

Sanford was fascinated by the urbane Mr. McGregor who displayed an unusual degree of calm in the circumstances. It seemed to Sanford that this man alone had the guts to tackle Britain's social ills and Sanford had listened to the rhetoric and seen a certain logic in aligning himself with McGregor; it would be a synergetic relationship.

At this point, Sanford made a decision to cross the line that he had walked faithfully for his whole Police career. The razor was sent for and Sanford examined it in private. There was blood on the handle that he did not doubt belonged to the complainant; he washed it off and dried the razor thoroughly. Next, he called for the prisoner to be brought into an interview room and their meeting was brief but memorable. The conversation was unrecorded and they were alone, which was also highly irregular.

Sanford seated himself at the interview table and addressed the prisoner in a friendly tone, "Mr McGregor, what can I do for you?"

McGregor replied, "Look, I know who you are and why you are here. I know that they stitched you up, but that doesn't have to be the end of it. Get me out of here, Sanford, drop these charges and I will never forget what you did for me"

Sanford pondered this briefly. He stood and paced the room, then coming close to McGregor he looked him in the eye and said carefully, "If you mean it, I will help you because I can see that you are someone who's going right to the top. Just don't forget your words, I'll do my part."

That was about the sum of it; the rest is history. Sanford recommended that McGregor be released and exonerated; there was insufficient evidence to accuse him. McGregor went on to win the Merseyside by-election by a landslide when his main opponent withdrew, citing family reasons. In the other wards contested by the Progress Party it was the same story in every election; candidates mysteriously withdrew from the race and the PP was elected virtually unopposed.

No one ever substantiated allegations of the participation of the PP in the riots that began later that year, but they were nationwide and the weakness of the Coalition Government was exposed. The Government lost a vote of confidence motion, which had been submitted by the Progress Party, and a General Election was called for.

McGregor's manifesto called for a strong government and promised solutions to the 'endemic rot' in British society. He was elected to Prime Minister following his Party's landslide victory in the following General Election. His first step was to declare a State of Emergency, and he suspended the Courts of Justice, replacing them with Tribunals that would judge under new emergency powers.

John Sanford received a call shortly after this to join McGregor in London. He was offered and accepted the new post of Minister of Public Security; his brief was to establish law and order under a new force to be called "The Defenders". The powers of the new force were not defined; it was for Sanford to redefine the laws in keeping with the manifesto of the Progress Party. He had been given a free hand to build a police state. This he did with ruthless efficiency.

Within thirty days, every member of the Selection Panel that had rejected Sanford's candidacy were arrested and charged with being 'enemies of the state' under the new Emergency Laws; they subsequently found themselves interned in a new prison in the Hebrides Islands, where they were put to hard labour. The conditions of confinement were damp and overcrowded, medical facilities fell far short of the normal standard and mortality rates among the elderly ex-chief constables was very high; only one survived after five years of imprisonment. This was to be the norm for opposition to the Progress Party's rule; some didn't even get the benefit of a trial, but were charged as 'being members of a terrorist organisation' and transferred to a maximum security prison, for 'observation'.

John Sanford now sat at his desk on the fiftieth floor of the Beehive Building, poring over the intelligence reports that were coming in about the infiltrations. He was also concerned about the unusual level of armed incidents in the past few days; why, in the Essex marshes someone had even planted a landmine which blew up a patrolling Defenders armoured car, then the survivors had been ruthlessly cut down by the ambushers!

This wasn't the only incident... all over the country there were explosions at government installations, roadside explosive devices were remotely activated, Defenders Stations were being ambushed by armed gangs; the list went on and on. Reports were also flooding in about hundreds of similar incidents all over the Euro Zone. The resources of the member governments were completely overstretched; he couldn't cope with this level of opposition. He needed the support of the Army and the other branches of the Armed Forces, but that was unlikely to be forthcoming, since he had arrested their top generals already. What was he supposed to do? Why were all of these incidents occurring now, all of a sudden?

He decided to focus on the itch that needed to be scratched; that guy of Astley Sinclair's. What was his name? Oh, yes, Stewart, Dr Jim Stewart. How come that Stewart couldn't figure out why these infiltrators were melting past his scanners? It had never happened before; and why now? There was something fishy going on with this guy!

He called for his aide and asked for the file on Dr Jim Stewart, technical consultant to the Cabinet. He also called for a drone to be despatched to monitor Stewart's residence in Somerset; let them enable thermal imaging scans and every imaginable device that would get him into that house remotely. His clerk, Sally, brought him the file.

Then he turned his attention to the Dutch reports. They had lost track of a woman and a boy in Amsterdam. They now believed that these were the same persons that had evaded the German Defenders; a barge operator was currently being interrogated to establish why he had carried two unauthorized passengers on his Rhine barge from Koblenz to Amsterdam.

Looking next at the map now spread out on the desktop, it was possible that the outbreak of armed incidents in the Essex marshes might be connected with a Defenders' surveillance report about a high speed boat in the vicinity of Tollesbury at about the same time that the mine went off. Could the two infiltrators have travelled up the Rhine to Amsterdam, and then hopped across the Channel to re-emerge in Essex? It seemed likely! If so, where were they headed? London was the obvious choice, but why, why? Too many questions and too much extrapolation based on a few facts! But Sanford's gut was telling him that he was right!

So his next call was to Operations where he ordered that roadblocks be set up around London, concentrating upon the East side and all arterial roads. He referred to the German Defenders report. Acting on his hunch, he ordered that a watch be made particularly for an Asian woman, of Japanese origin and a Eurasian child about four years of age. If these infiltrators thought that they would evade John Sanford's net, they were to be disappointed!

The objects of Sanford's roadblocks were by this time safely past North London Super Dome. Andrew was receiving constant updates about the checkpoints over the radio from the Angel's network of local agents. It seemed that the Defenders were stretched thin, and could only manage to set up their roadblocks on the arterial roads. It was a simple matter therefore to take the minor roads around the checkpoints; for good measure, the Angels mounted grenade attacks upon the checkpoints so that the Defenders' focus would remain upon the main roads. By dawn, they were through Watford and it was time for a welcome break and a change of car. Someone in the local Angels had thought about a hot meal so they hungrily ate from the hot wrapped sandwiches and drank tea from the flasks that they had brought along.

By ten o'clock they were well on their way to the West Country. Passing through Andover without incident, again thanks to the protecting Angels, they headed for Warminster where they changed cars again and then it was cross country via Shepton Mallet until they finally entered the small city of Wells, Somerset.

Wells happens to be the smallest city in England. It is a quiet market town lying beneath the sheltering Mendip Hills. It also boasts the fine monument of Wells Cathedral, which dates back to the thirteenth century. There are numerous ancient Roman artefacts for tourists to visit, including the renowned bubbling springs of water, which was perhaps what attracted the Romans to the area.

The rendezvous with Bill Stewart was fixed to be in front of the Cathedral, on Sadler Street, which borders Cathedral Green. Even at that time of the year, a few tourists wandered around the ancient city centre; no one would think it remarkable that a Japanese lady and a small child would be parked in front of the main tourist attraction.

At twelve o'clock the Cathedral clock chimed out the hour and Bill's ground car rolled into the Green. Everyone was so happy to meet up, but as Andrew was anxious to be on his way, they had to cut short the introductions and change cars for the final time.

They exited the Green down College Street, heading for Priddy. It was fortunate that they were so quick in the transfer, because two minutes later, as Andrew left in the opposite direction, he passed a Defenders patrol vehicle that entered Cathedral Green and stopped in the pedestrian way in front of the Cathedral, where the Patrol immediately began scrutinizing ID's of every passer-by, especially harassing the tourists; it was only routine.

The ground car slipped out of Wells, its occupants blissfully unaware of the confrontation that they had so narrowly missed. There was so much to see and Bill kept up a running commentary all the way to the farm. On the way, he made sure to make a short detour so that they could see the Priddy Circles.

Bill explained for Akiyoshi's benefit as much as he knew about the ancient British people called Celts who had erected the huge Circle's stones and wooden posts, having transported them all the way from South Wales; overland south at first, and then they probably floated them on pontoons or rafts along the South Wales coast, and then across the waters of the Bristol Channel and up the rivers until they arrived on site at Priddy. Once they reached Priddy, an army of slaves laboured to erect the henge so that it stood perfectly aligned with other monuments along the length of Britain. He told also about the Druids, the priests who ruled the Celts, and with some embellishments, he spoke of the gory sacrifices that they'd offered on that very spot. Akiyoshi was fascinated and wanted to know more, but Bill could only explain what he as an engineer could imagine had been the engineering problems that such a technology-poor culture had had to overcome with innovative solutions and force of numbers.

In the end he concluded by saying, "Maybe they weren't so primitive after all, any more than the ancient Egyptians were; we are still figuring out just how the Pyramids were built. But we do know that the neighbouring people, the Phoenicians, used to trade for copper and tin with the Celts of Cornwall, so maybe there was some technology transfer going on?"

They turned into the Farm's drive and once again the avenue of Japanese cherry trees drew delighted approval from his oriental guests; the blossoms were beginning to open as the warmth of a late April Spring broke through the damp winter airs; the sight of the pink and white flowers was already beautiful, soon they would be breathtaking!

Hearing the crunch of the gravel on the driveway, Grace and Sakura came flying out of the Cottage. They threw their arms around Asuka and Akiyoshi, hugged them and then jumped up and down in their excitement at being reunited. After a short while, John and Bill managed to get everyone inside again. They explained that a drone observer unit had been spotted in the vicinity, so it would be best if they stayed indoors for a while. Soon Akiyoshi and Grace went exploring the room downstairs. Like any four-year-olds, they ran excitedly up and down the rooms and the tunnels that connected the cottages. Occasionally, like a couple of rabbits emerging from a rabbit hole, they would pop up in one of the other cottages, and then disappear only to re-emerge elsewhere. They never seemed to tire of this game, which was just as well as it kept them amused while the adults conversed about their adventures.

Asuka related how she had travelled up the Rhine with Akiyoshi, and ruefully showed her bruises from the skimmer's charge across the Channel. They all laughed. Everyone was encouraged, however, as she told them about the umbrella of protection that the Angels had provided them all the way. Andrew had also kept them informed about what the Angels were doing across the country by way of diversions. Everyone was thrilled to hear of this because the media were characteristically silent about what was *really* going on. Some of the explosions were put down to gas leaks, but later, because there were just too many incidents to be covered by that story, a new spin on the story announced that Asian infiltrators were attacking Euro Zone governments, trying to destabilize their blessed Union.

Alone on the hillside above the farm, the watcher sent in his report; asset number two had been safely delivered. He also mentioned that a drone aircraft was circling the farm, presumably making scans; he requested instructions. In a few minutes, in another burst of condensed radio traffic, Angel Headquarters ordered him to take out the drone. He focussed his laser sight on the drone's propulsion unit. The pulsed laser bored a hole straight through the drone and it dropped like a stone into the fields. He sent an acknowledgment to the Angels controller with the coordinates of the drone's location so that it could be retrieved. Ten minutes later, a farm tractor was hauling the carcass of the drone across the fields. It was eventually towed to the site of a sink hole and it disappeared without trace.

In London, Sanford was informed about the loss of his drone. He cursed for a while with some choice Merseyside expletives and then, after he had vented his frustration, he requested the controllers to send him whatever data they had received from the drone before it was lost. The stills images were not very informative, but what did intrigue him was the video showing the thermal imaging inside the cottages.

He referred to the Stewart file. According to the file, Jim Stewart lived with his two brothers in the three cottages. There were no servants, no pets, just a few sheep and cattle which were kept in pens or left to graze on the hills around the farmhouses; so what were those other thermal images that moved around the central cottage? He could clearly see not three but four adult images and what looked like two children. Very strange!

Now he knew that Stewart had taken off from Yeovilton on a Scranton Jump Jet, just hours ago, in fact he had authorized the mission himself; so who were the other two adults? Sanford felt a sense of excitement building... the good Dr Stewart was up to something; just what, Sanford didn't know yet, but he was going to find out.

He picked up the phone and called Major Hinckley in Defenders Surveillance Department. "Major, Sanford here. Look, I've got a job for you. It's something that you need to attend to personally, a very urgent and sensitive matter you understand…"

In Sanford's outer office, Sally cleared the coffee cups and generally acted as general factotum for everybody else. She was invisible as she went about her duties; her black hair was tied back in a spinster's bun, her thick last century spectacles gave her a somewhat owlish look, and her shapeless form went totally ignored as she shuffled from desk to desk.

Her stupid look was engineered, of course, in actual fact Sally held a Masters Degree in Computer Sciences and was fluent in three languages. Right now, thanks to Sally, what Sanford was looking at on his terminal was being simultaneously viewed on the terminal of Jack Bailey, of the UK Angels Network.

"Oh everyone!" Bailey exclaimed. "We have a thermal image of Stewart's farmhouse here, you can clearly see the children running about. It must have been that damned drone! Phil, we need to get ready for visitors and prepare for an evacuation if necessary!" He reached for his comm. link, "Sally, I think that Mr. Sanford is about to go down with a nasty virus, kindly arrange it!"

The watcher was duly informed to expect visitors. He was to act as a backup to the Angels Response Team and make sure that no visitor left alive.

Chapter Nine: Visitors

Bill's comm. link buzzed. An unsigned text message, sender's number unknown! The message said simply, "Expect unwelcome visitors soon!" What no one knew was that the brothers had planned for just such an event as this. Some might call it paranoia, but Jim had dealt with many unsavoury people in the course of his missions around the world. He had made many enemies too; people that wouldn't think twice about killing everyone on sight if they gained entry to his home.

Bill sounded the alarm and he and John swung into action like a well-oiled machine. All papers were sent down to the vault downstairs by vacuum transfer. All traces of their visitors' presence were carefully cleaned away. Finally, Bill opened the floor panel and they all descended to the lower vaulted room. Here, he armed the self-defence system and now there remained only evacuation for all of them. They squeezed into the three capsules and the automatic launch sequence was initiated. The capsules dropped into the tubes one after another and the tubes were sealed closed automatically after their exit. The doorway to the lower room remained open as intended, welcoming their unwelcome visitors.

A little while later, the capsules reached the safety point at the end of the escape tubes. Everyone was well although a bit shaken up. John turned on the video monitors at his remote control centre, which gave him an internal view of the cottages and an external coverage of the farmyard and animal pens.

Perhaps five minutes after the warning, they heard the proximity alarms announcing the arrival, by air and road, of the Defenders. A team of ten Defenders peeled out of the rotor turbo vehicle and four more came from the armoured ground vehicle. They seemed surprised to find the front door open and even more so that there was a hidden stairway leading down to a large room, which appeared to be a laboratory. The cottage was evidently deserted.

"Someone must have warned them," muttered Major Hinckley. He ordered his men to all go down into the laboratory and to remove any records that they found there, which they duly did.

To his great amazement, after they had descended to the lab, the floor panel silently resealed itself. He searched frantically for the control that would reopen the floor panel but to no avail. Actually, since the system was now being remotely controlled by John, he couldn't have opened it anyway.

Meanwhile outside, the watcher had efficiently silenced the driver of the armoured vehicle and the rotor turbo vehicle's pilot, both with a single shot to the head. Realizing that he had been caught in a trap, Hinckley rushed for the door, only to meet the same fate as his pilot.

At the same time in the laboratory below ground, the self defence system pumped a mixture of lethal gases into the now sealed room. Death was instantaneous, and there were no survivors.

John activated the pumps to evacuate the toxic air and the robot cleaners performed the programmed cleanup operation for the bodies.

Within ten minutes, the ghastly scene had resumed normalcy and the meters indicated that the air had now returned to breathable levels. The small party of adults and children exited the tunnel and began the walk back to the farm.

The sun was shining. A lark rose from the field; its shrill song filled the sky, and birds sang in the trees below. No one would have thought that such a massacre could have occurred on such a beautiful afternoon.

As they reached the farm, they were just in time to see the rotor turbo vehicle and the armoured vehicle leave the farm; the Angels Response Team was doing salvage and a cleanup too.

Jack Bailey was delighted at the acquisition of the Defenders' hardware. It would come in very useful, as would the guns and laser rifles that the watcher had spotted neatly stacked outside the farmhouse door that afternoon. Quite what happened to the posse of men who had disappeared inside the Stewart Farm, he couldn't guess, but he figured that wherever they were now, they certainly wouldn't need those weapons anymore! A cleanup detail removed them silently while the family sat at their midday meal.

Chapter Ten: Eluding the Hunters

The E.A.R. agents followed the Russians down the road from Hendek. Their lights dimmed, they played a cat and mouse game with the other team. The Russians turned into the large crowded car park of Sabika Gokcen Havaalani International Airport and the Chinese slipped unobtrusively into the far side of the car park where they might see but not be seen.

The Russians walked into the Departures area; several flights were due to depart within the hour but boarding was already starting for two of them. They looked around for some vantage point where they might be able to view the boarding passengers. On an upper floor a cleaner was working in an office that overlooked the concourse and the departure gates; that would do just fine.

They walked quickly to the stairs, which were manned by a security guard. Hardly breaking step, the guard was despatched with a stiletto to the heart. It was a neat professional blow and he hardly made a noise as he looked down to see a small circle of blood staining his chest. They carefully removed him from his stool and placed him behind the desk. None of the milling crowd saw anything. No one would see the corpse for some time.

Once upstairs they entered the office that was their target. The cleaner was bending over the robotic cleaning machine; something had gone wrong with it again. A knife slash across his windpipe silenced him permanently and he collapsed in a heap.

The hunters surveyed the scene below. The gates were crowded with passengers anxiously shoving each other trying to board.

"Out of control as usual, damn Turks!" There were no foreigners to be seen, except a couple of elderly black people who didn't match the targets' descriptions.

"OK, so now what? Do we go back now?" "Look," the leader said, "see that Chinese guy down there? I am betting that he is E.A.R., you don't see them quitting do you?" He consulted the wall map in the office, "See here, there is a small airfield just north of here, maybe seventy kilometres only... we will go there, if that's a bust then you can go back to your precious Istanbul nightclubs!" They all laughed, it was common knowledge that the butt of their humour had fallen for one of the belly dancers in their favourite club; he would be first through the door when it opened! They exited the office, stepping casually over the dead cleaner's corpse.

As they left the Departures Hall there was a scream; someone had found the guard. This was shortly followed by a second scream; that must be the cleaner. Time to leave!

The Chinese observed the Russians' departure. Their colleague hastily rejoined them.

"Quick, let's go! They've killed two people inside. There will be cops all over us in a minute and we won't be able to get out then!"

The E.A.R. car tore out of the car park, its wheels spinning on the ungravelled surface. As they left the car park, the Turkish Police were quickly mobilizing and a cordon had already been placed about the Departures Hall. They turned north, in pursuit now of the Russians, because they surely had some definite intelligence to work on, so the race was on!

The Scranton Jump Jet circled Cengiz Topel Naval Air Station, Kocaali, waiting for landing permission. Eventually the Duty Officer gave the all clear for landing.

Dr Jim's Autopilot passed Jim's instructions; "This is a classified flight on Euro Zone Cabinet business. The aircraft will land away from the military zone in order to load cargo from one of the civilian hangars. No assistance is required. Do not approach the aircraft. Is this instruction clear?"

The Duty Officer hastily gave consent and Jim made one more circuit of the Airfield just to make sure that there were no intruders that might spoil his plan.

It was good that he did so. Below him, he could see the main gates to the Civilian Area. Two cars were stationary at the gate. As he watched, several muzzle flashes, like those of old technology automatic machine guns, lit up the gateway and then one of the cars burst through the gates, heading for the civilian hangars. It was starting to look as if he was just too late!

The car stopped at the first hangar and two men peeled out to check; presumably the hangar was bare because they jumped back into the car and drove to the next hangar, where the car came screeching to a halt. This time all four of the hunters, for that was what Jim guessed they must be, entered the hangar.

Inside the hangar, the trio of Gabriel, Ren and Akemi huddled beneath a tarpaulin. The feet of the Chinese assassins approached them confidently.

Suddenly Ren stood up and addressed them in Mandarin Chinese, "Who are you and why are you following us?

"Oh my dear," the team leader replied sarcastically, "Greetings from my master, Chen Li."

"You can keep your greetings," Ren replied boldly, "and answer my question immediately!"

"Well, I have an invitation for you. Come with us now or your body will be food for the Turkish vultures!"

At this point the voice of a child entered the conversation, and Akemi stood in front of her mother. "Mummy, are these men going to hurt you?"

The man interjected, "Little girl, I'm afraid that that is correct; and I will also kill her, and you, and that Arab behind you!"

"No, I won't let you," she said firmly, her small feet squarely set as if she was about to land a punch. The assassins had a good laugh at this; it was ludicrous coming from such a little one. Pity she had to die too!

Then something strange began to happen. The men began to shake and cry out in terror. They began firing wildly at each other, all the while shouting, "Bear, bear!"

Soon the last of the E.A.R. agents crumpled to the ground, shot by his own men.

"Akemi, what did you do?" shouted a terrified Gabriel.

"Oh, I just made them afraid. They thought that the others were bears who were attacking them, that's why they fired at each other!"

Just at that moment they heard the deafening blast of the Scranton Jump Jet outside the hangar and, as they opened the doors, there it was facing them, looking malevolent and primed to fire into the hangar.

Jim couldn't believe his eyes, here they were, calm as you like walking towards him and behind them a mound of bodies. Surely these must be the last of the assassins?

He immediately killed the engines and the jet settled on the tarmac. He jumped down and ran to the trio. "You, I know," he said addressing Gabriel, "I shall be forever in your debt! But you two, I only know by reputation! You are Ren and you are Akemi, I presume? Look, this cover of mine may not last for long; let's talk on the way to England. Gabriel, you'd best be going too, there's another pile of bodies at the gate. This place is going to be crawling with Military Police in a few minutes, so sooner rather than later, eh pal? Oh yes, the funds have been wired to your bank account; I'll expect that you will be more than satisfied."

The jet lifted off within a few minutes, just as Gabriel's car cleared the main gates. From the other side of the field, the Military Police were hurtling across the open space to the gates to see what had been going on. It had indeed been a close call!

Chapter Eleven: Flying Blind

A little after four o'clock Sanford's system restarted by itself, and his computer gurus were baffled... had they been hacked? An hour later, the entire Defenders' computer system was down again, but worse still, all of the backups of the system had mysteriously been corrupted. The very eyes and ears of the Defenders had been shut. Even worse, a virus had entered the archived records and now the video footage and textual records were totally unreadable. Thousands of cameras and scanners around Britain simply could not communicate what they were scanning; it was a total disaster, as far as Sanford was concerned. No one could figure out just how the hackers had gained access to such a high level security system!

Minutes after the second computer shutdown, a transformed Sally simply walked out of the Bee Hive; gone was the spinster's bun and the pebble glasses, and the metres of padding that had encircled her waistline were now reposing in a waste bin on the fiftieth floor. The curvaceous young lady who left the building carried a new identity; her RFID showed her name as "Betty Crocker, Food Nutritionist to the Cabinet Office"; a wry stab of humour that was completely lost on the moron at the gate who was forced to check every ID manually.

For some reason, Sanford connected Stewart with his troubles. He connected with Yeovilton Base and spoke with the Base Commander. He revoked the air rights of Stewart and asked him to dispatch some Interceptors.

"This man has to be stopped at all costs," he ranted, "do whatever it takes, and I want him eliminated!"

"Yes, sir," replied Jim's old friend, "I'll see that he gets the message alright!" Sanford looked at the comm. link quizzically for a moment, then closed the line with his usual, "Sanford, out!"

The next action by the Base Commander was to go and make himself a cup of tea. He needed time to think! After a little while, he had decided upon a course of action that would cover his butt while protecting Jim's.

Shortly after this, Jim's comm. link received a terse message from his old friend in Ops, Yeovilton. It read, "Granny isn't what she used to be!"

It was an old code that they'd used in the Unit; it referred to the story of Little Miss Riding Hood. Jim knew now that his cover had been blown. Well, if he couldn't go to Granny's house, he'd have to take the Scranton to his house instead! Let's see what Sanford would make of that!

As a precaution against Interceptors, he'd already masked the aircraft's transponder, so he was now basically invisible unless someone caught him on radar. To prevent that happening, Jim then ordered the Auto Pilot to drop the Scranton to ten metres above sea level. Still travelling at Mach two point five, the jet screamed over the sea, homeward bound; thank God for Artificial

Intelligence now! One tiny slip or air pocket and a human reaction time would be just too slow to prevent disaster. He reprogrammed the destination into the computer and the Auto Pilot reconfigured itself to fly to Priddy.

"This ought to be quite an entrance," Jim mused.

The watcher on the hill could hardly believe his eyes. He was so shocked that he broke radio silence. "You'll never guess what he's brought home now!" he breathed into his mouthpiece, "a bloody fighter plane, that's what!"

It seemed that Angel HQ was also at a loss for words, but after a slight pause, there came a laconic "Stand by."

Within an hour Jim's comm. link rang. The caller ID was blank, but Jim had a fairly good idea whom it might be.

"Good afternoon, Dr Stewart. I think we should meet, would you be willing?"

"Yes, indeed; you see I appear to have crossed the Rubicon. For me there's no turning back now!" replied Jim, "and I wonder whether you could arrange some valet parking for my transportation which is parked outside my cottage, as I'm sure you are aware?"

"Yes, quite," the caller said, "even as we speak; I'll be in touch very soon."

Outside the sound of the Scranton lifting off shattered the calm of the afternoon, and then it was gone; somewhere safe Jim hoped.

Chapter Twelve: Angels All About You

John Sanford was reduced to any form of communications that did not require the assistance of a computer; he could not send as much as a text message from his desktop. All he could see on his screen was a cartoon of an angel with a ludicrously enlarged grin, bobbing up and down and making obscene gestures, it turned around and dropped its pants and grinned lasciviously at him.

"It's outrageous and disgusting!" he ranted... "How dare they?"

His comm. link, fortunately, was operated by an independent system and now it was signalling him. There was a General Harvey from Southern Army Command GHQ calling him; now what?

"Yes, General, to what do I owe this pleasure?" Sanford asked in his politest tone.

"Sir, I doubt that this call will give you any pleasure... do you know what is going on outside the Bee Hive?" General Harvey asked. It was a question asked in such a way that demanded an answer. The impertinence of the man, thought Sanford, does he know to whom he is speaking?

"General," he replied, with a hard edge now to his voice, "we are in control of the situation. Just having a few technical difficulties, that's all. It's merely temporary."

"I'm not sure what you're talking about, Mr Sanford. I am speaking about a missing rotor turbo vehicle, an armoured car and a Scranton

Jump Jet; all of which are fully armed and apparently not in your possession, but in the hands of the rebel forces known as the Angels Network." The General replied somewhat testily. "I repeat my question; sir, do you know what is going on outside the Bee Hive? And, I might also ask, Are you in control of the situation?"

John Sanford staggered in shock at the import of the General's news, and he was more than a little nervous about the implication of this Senior Staff Officer's second question.

"General," Sanford blustered, "I assume that you realize the consequences of a confrontation with me?"

The General was not to be so easily intimidated, however. "Sanford, you are in no position to be making threats to the Staff Officers of GHQ! At the moment we are watching the situation throughout the country, and indeed the Euro Zone. In case you require me to spell it out for you, there is an armed insurrection going on... and you cannot deal with it alone. Now what I am asking you is this; are you prepared to hand over your Emergency Powers to the Armed Forces? We are not prepared to sit on our hands while the country descends into anarchy and you just stand there pissing in your pants from fear!"

For the second time in the conversation, Sanford staggered. Oh, boy! This was his worst nightmare coming to pass! "General, I will have to consult with the Prime Minister and get back to you!"

"Well, don't take too long!" General Harvey replied. "You have a short window of opportunity." With that final salvo, General Harvey closed the link.

Sanford mopped his brow and loosened his collar. What had Stewart done? Had he given the Scranton Jump Jet to the terrorist Angels Network... unbelievable! Then the realization that his fortress was under siege now and his closely guarded secrets might all come tumbling out into the open caused him to break out into another profuse bout of sweating. He decided that he would have to see McGregor personally about the latest developments.

As Sanford made his way by the lift from the fiftieth floor to McGregor's office on the sixtieth, he was not aware of what was an even more serious development about to take place ten floors below him.

The Scranton was poised outside the windows of Sanford's office, like a malevolent avenging angel. Its heavy calibre guns were lined up on the deserted office's interior.

The jet was under remote control and the controllers kept the Jet's cameras rolling as they unleashed a devastating rain of fire upon the building. The heavy shells sprayed across the floor-to-ceiling syntho-glass windows, shattering them into thousands of shards, and tore off the now-shredded alloy façade of the building, sending a cascade of debris plummeting to the street below. The furniture inside the office was reduced to splinters and the very structure of the building shuddered under the barrage of fire.

The whole event lasted perhaps two minutes, but there was now a gaping space where the fiftieth floor used to be. The object lesson was over; the Scranton slowly backed away and then accelerated low over the city, doing a victory roll over Buckingham Palace as it left.

On the sixtieth floor, the two most powerful men in Britain crouched, absolutely terrified, behind the desk of the Prime Minister; as if that would have afforded them any protection from a repeat performance from the Scranton's guns. The frame of the building whined under the stress applied by the assault it had just endured, but the structure somehow survived it. For several minutes neither could speak. What had happened was so awesome, so totally beyond their wildest nightmares that their minds were spinning in shock.

Finally, McGregor was able to get his question out, "What, what was that?" Sanford told him about General Harvey's call.

On the Stewart Farm they were celebrating the reunion of Ren and Akiyoshi with the others. The children jubilantly joined hands and they danced around the room, leaping and jumping as they laughed in their delight. It was contagious; soon the three brothers and the cousins joined in the merriment. They had passed through many dangers and now they were safe for the moment anyway!

Jim's comm. link buzzed; another text from the anonymous caller, "Switch on your media screens, any channel will do!"

Jim hurriedly gave the voice command to the house system and the screens all came alive with the breaking news of an attack upon the Bee Hive Building itself. Both from the cockpit and nearby buildings, the cameras had captured the destruction of John Sanford's entire floor by the Scranton's cannons. The news anchors carried a statement from the Angel Network claiming responsibility for the attack and promising that there would be a series of escalating attacks upon the so-called icons of the Ian McGregor regime until they agreed to rescind the Emergency Powers Decree. Everyone in the cottage stood stunned; such a thing had never happened during the entire dictatorial reign of McGregor.

There followed a brief statement by a Government spokesman claiming that a group of subversives, aided by East Asian infiltrators, were trying to destabilize the great United Kingdom but already the Defenders were rounding up the ringleaders and the emergency would very soon be history.

They further stated that the Armed Forces would be moving into position to protect public buildings and institutions and to prevent any such incidents again. The statement was followed by the National Anthem and some film footage showing King Charles the Fourth smiling and waving to his subjects; he was accompanied by The Right Honourable Ian McGregor and some members of the Cabinet also waving from the balcony of Buckingham Palace. The segment cut to a picture of the Union Jack fluttering as a background to a parade of the Defenders marching in full uniform; it was old library footage, taken at least a year ago on National Defence Day.

The comm. link buzzed again; "We should meet, tomorrow morning at your farm. Don't worry, there are Angels all around you!" Jim silently showed the message to the other adults. John said, "I'll put the kettle on, looks as if we need a cup of tea after this!"

Chapter Thirteen: A Council of War

In contrast to the levity of a few moments ago, everyone now had become very serious. Sakura started the discussion.

"I think we can safely assume that we are all now quite close to the top of McGregor's Most Wanted List. That is to say, we don't get to choose which side we are on, or whether we will get involved; we are involved and we have to be with the Angels."

Jim nodded in agreement. "Well, yes, they started this; they were the ones who declared war on us! But they definitely didn't expect to get their noses bloodied in this way!"

Bill joined the discussion, "Let's analyze what that statement didn't have — they mentioned the Armed Forces support, but nowhere was there a single image of the High Command. Does that mean anything, everyone?"

John frowned and rubbed his chin, then added, "Well it's an open question, still to be answered either way. My guess is that the Armed Forces are still sitting on the fence and waiting to see what leverage they can place upon Ian McGregor."

"Well," Asuka said, "The internal politics we don't understand, but the symbolism was unmistakeable — they wheeled that poor old King out and played patriotic music to bolster their image, they are trying to say 'look we are the good guys, they are the bad guys who are trying to tear down the great British way of life!'"

Ren agreed, "Yes, a way of life under the jack-booted heels of the Defenders! Notice the symbolism of the marching Defenders – all designed to portray unity and strength."

Jim nodded in agreement. "OK, so there are some questions about the position of the Armed Forces, the Government has been badly shaken by this and they are in the midst of damage control, which judging by the rapidity of the production of that propaganda film, means that they are regrouping. If they can show the Armed Forces that they are still able to govern, my guess is that the Armed Forces will hold off on their own power play. But for how long will they hold off?"

Sakura added her thought to Jim's, "Perhaps that question may be answered by our visitor tomorrow... do we know who he is?"

Jim replied, "My best guess... it will be the leader of the Angels, or a highly placed deputy. I've heard whispers that they are led by a man called 'Jack Bailey', but no one knows if that's his true name. He rarely ventures out in public, I'm told."

Bill tapped on the table firmly with his index finger, to emphasize his question, "Irrespective of *who* comes, *what* do we think he's coming for? I hope that it's to tell us what they are planning and what part we all are to play in their plans."

Asuka agreed and added, "Well, let's not forget something, the resistance movements have invested heavily in one thing only — to bring three children across the world; they have shadowed our every move, provided food and shelter, placed an umbrella of protection about us all the way. It's not about us, Bill, it's about the children. They need the children, not us. We are only incidental in their great plan, whatever that might be. If they need the children, then it's because of the talents and abilities that they uniquely possess!"

Ren nodded emphatically. "My sister is right, this all about KP!"

"Indeed," said John, "In which case, and I'm sure that we all agree you are correct, we have to safeguard the children's interests primarily. We can't have some gung ho resistance leader putting them in the way of danger!"

Jim summed up the council's consensus, "OK, that's agreed all around! Now when Mr. Angel comes calling we shall all be present, and we shall push for answers to these questions."

The following morning it rained. The clouds just opened and the downpour looked as if it might continue through the day. It was only the intruder alarms ringing that warned them of the arrival of their guests, the driveway was sodden and muffled the sounds of wheels until the cars reached the house. Jim considerately took out umbrellas for his guests.

There were four men. Two carried laser weapons with a second gun over the shoulder; clearly they were taking no chances. A slightly built man stepped forward and offered his hand.

"Hi, I'm Jack Bailey and this is my deputy, Phil Meredith." He didn't introduce the other two men, who seemed to be bodyguards. Jim asked them to come in out of the rain and they all stepped inside.

Jim made the introductions to the adults and then brought out the children: Akiyoshi, Akemi and then Grace. "It is an honour to meet you all, thank you for agreeing to see us," Jack stated. "I think that you are all incredibly brave," he added. "Would you take some tea? We will sit over here where it will be more comfortable to talk," Jim answered.

Soon the tea was served in man-sized mugs and Jack and Phil gently steamed dry in front of the farmhouse's Inglenook fireplace.

"My! I can't remember when I last saw a real fire in a house," Jack exclaimed. "How do you do it?"

Jim explained, "We discovered a lot of old wooden props and roofing materials when we were renovating the old mine workings beneath the cottage. We fitted a chemical scrubber to the flue and we recycle the heat back into the house for water heating and the solar panels provide the rest of our electrical needs for the three cottages. We have a minimal ecological impact, so no eco-inspectors would have reason to disturb us here!"

"It's very comfortable, I must say," Bailey enthused. "Now if you don't mind I would like to come directly to the point. Our visit today is two-fold: first to express our thanks for the armaments that you have so generously donated to The Angels Network; as you have seen they are being put to very good use. Secondly, to explain why we have brought these three young ladies and their children all the way from Japan to England. Without a doubt, this mission will change the world!"

"The Angels Network is merely one of a worldwide collaboration between democratic national movements that want an end to the present power bloc system and a return to a free United Nations forum where everyone will have a voice and a right to self determination. The Euro Zone, E.A.R. and the Russian Federation are merely an aberration; their time must pass, the despots will fall. We are not merely reinstituting a failed organisation in the U.N., because it did fail us; but the very basis of society, of mankind, will need to be changed too… I speak, of course, of KP!"

At the mention of KP there was a gasp of surprise around the room. "Jack," Jim asked, "We know the abilities of KP, but how do you expect to change the 'very basis of society'? We expected that it would take generations for the modified DNA to spread throughout the human gene pool."

"Quite simply, it is because we have synthesized KP! It is now colourless, tasteless and of course odourless. It is also soluble in water. The modified KP is even more powerful than the original which was developed by Dr Toshio Hokaida and Dr Glenda Woods, but we are seeing only phase two symptoms in the adults that volunteered to be our guinea pigs. We lack the expertise to do the embryonic transfer of enhancement that Drs Hokaida and Woods achieved. Dr Woods, by the way, is alive and well in Japan, and under the protection of the Japanese

111

Underground. These children, however, have the knowledge inherent for the development of the enhancement programme, but for our immediate needs, the introduction of the synthetic KP into the world's populations by ingestion will suffice."

"Wow!" Sakura exclaimed, "Are you serious? This is massive, so important!"

"Well, your mother thought so too. She, principally, was the inventor of the synthetic KP." Bailey smiled.

Then, turning to Jim, he addressed him, "Dr Jim Stewart, you also have some talents that we may put to good use. You are an expert in the technology of the scanners now in use by most security organizations, especially in the UK, by the Defenders?" Jim nodded, knowing what was coming next. "Would you be able to deactivate the scanners remotely, Dr Jim?

Jim replied, "You know, many people would die for the answer to that question, and until yesterday when Sanford's thugs burst into my home intent upon killing my children... well, I would have lied and told you, 'no, it's not possible.' But it is possible, and in fact I have already engineered a little black box that can do just that! In fact, as you stand leaning on my fireplace your hand rests upon the solution to your question!"

Bailey jumped as if the fire had somehow leapt out and scalded his hand! "What? You have already solved the problem that we have been working on for years! Why didn't I come calling earlier?"

"It wouldn't have done you much good," Jim replied truthfully. "Now there are limitations; it's line of sight basically, everything within a five hundred metre line of sight can be deactivated. It's also untraceable; scanners and x-rays will not detect its circuitry, it looks exactly like a comm. link, like any kid might carry." Jim concluded, nonchalantly, "You could easily fit it into any shell you wish, I suppose."

"How many of these do you have Dr. Stewart?" Bailey asked, eagerly.

Jim replied, "Call me Jim, Jack. Just a few, maybe five for now, but we have all of the parts and a robotic assembly line downstairs in the lab… probably we might be able to make a hundred, more, if you can get me the parts I need and the shell casings. Here, take that one. I'll give you two more too. Test them for yourself, and then let me know what you think about my 'descanner'."

"Indeed I will! This is amazing, quite a bonus, we never thought we would find such a prize in addition to the children's talents. The whole world is going to be just as excited. Will it work on all brands of scanner?"

"Er, no," Jim replied, "It may have limited success with some brands, but I will give your techies the algorithms that ought to enable them to tailor-make descanners for every situation; at the least they could jam the scanners whilst they passed through the zone." Bailey rose to leave and concluded saying, "Excellent, excellent! Please proceed with the fabrication of the other descanners, I will obtain the parts you need. We are in such a great hurry; our deadline is before May the First! Wonderful to meet you all, and we will stay in touch."

"I will send you the data file for the parts with schematics for your procurement needs. Just send me a message with a secure number and I'll do my part," promised Jim.

Chapter Fourteen: Escalation

On April fifteenth, a man walked into the most secure area of the Justice Tribunal Building, and entered the records rooms where current cases are temporarily stored. He selected and then removed certain case files from the vault, carefully placed them in his briefcase and simply walked out. No one thought about stopping him, it was assumed that the tag attached to his chest gave him the required clearances.

Five minutes later, the entire records for all current cases under action by the Justice Tribunal in Central London area were destroyed by a fire that the fire prevention system was unable to extinguish. Simultaneously, in the Birmingham and Manchester Tribunals' records vaults, the exact same thing occurred. Dr Jim's descanner passed its field test with flying colours.

Sanford was incredulous and demanded to know just how it had been engineered. His technicians admitted that all systems had been compromised for approximately ten minutes but had mysteriously returned to service apparently none the worse for their sleep; they also informed him that in every case the scanners were of the Stewart brand. The trouble was, only Dr Stewart would be able to solve the problem and in the circumstances he was most unlikely to cooperate.

Sanford immediately ordered a tightening of security procedures at every checkpoint. Henceforth, a manual verification was mandatory in addition to the automatic scan; this was, he reflected, locking the stable door after the horse had bolted.

He decided that he would go down to Priddy himself. He would see Stewart alone and convince him that 'for the good of the country, let's let bygones be bygones'. Yes, that was the best way, surely Stewart would be reasonable if he thought that there was no accounting for the Scranton jet incident… but Sanford's memory was long and he definitely would get his revenge; he would get his own back!

On April sixteenth, just before sunset, a Defenders' armoured car rolled down New Horizons Avenue and came to a halt outside the Central Treasury building. It was an imposing building of syntho-glass and alloy construction, which shone like a mirror reflecting the rays of the setting sun. The vehicle approached the main entrance and the darkened windows of bullet-proof glass concealed whoever might be inside.

Building security personnel approached the armoured vehicle; after the Justice Tribunal incident everybody was subject to close scrutiny, including the Defenders themselves. The sergeant on duty approached the driver's door and knocked.

"Please identify yourself," he ordered. There was no reply from within. He repeated his command, this time grasping the door control with his free hand while he drew his hand weapon with the other hand.

He immediately received a high voltage electric shock from the vehicle's anti-personnel self-defence device. The vehicle, which was robotically controlled, swivelled its main weapon, a fifty-millimetre cannon, and commenced firing. The target area appeared to be right above the doors of the main entrance and was in the shape of two large triangular holes that spanned a distance of twenty metres and joined at one corner near the base.

Everything within the triangles was removed methodically by the robotic gunner. The shelling continued unabated until every trace of the original façade of the building had been obliterated within the shapes. Upon completion of his design, the robot reversed his vehicle away from the building, narrowly missing the luckless sergeant who lay supine upon the steps of the Treasury.

There, in the clearest message sent yet, the motif of the Angels had been engraved over the entrance to the Treasury; the Angels had stamped their claim upon the wealth of the United Kingdom of Great Britain.

The Defenders were quick to rally and poured a hail of fire upon the armoured vehicle as it progressed back along the way it had come. However, for good measure, covering fire was then provided by a Defenders' rotor turbo vehicle that had suddenly appeared as if from nowhere. A barrage of rocket fire and heavy cannon now rained upon the Defenders, who scattered, looking for cover. The armoured vehicle was never found, most likely because the Angels had arranged for a heavy lift vehicle, waiting just around the corner, to whisk it away in minutes, covered by a tarpaulin emblazoned with the Defenders logo.

All around London Central in the rest of that week, there were hit and run incidents of a similar sort; sometimes a man with a shoulder mounted rocket launcher would fire at a government building and then melt away in the crowd; at other times it was grenades or remotely controlled explosive devices; always the target was the Government or the Defenders themselves. The pressure was unrelenting; who could blame the Defenders for believing that they were under siege? For that was exactly what Jack Bailey and his Angels intended. They meant to demoralize the rank and file of the Defenders to the point of desertion.

Under such pressure, who could blame John Sanford for a momentary lapse in judgement? He ordered his bodyguard to stand down and took his private flying vehicle on an undisclosed flight plan, his destination: Priddy, Somerset.

In the farmhouse they were alerted by the proximity alarms of the arrival of a flying vehicle. All within the farmhouse went on alert, except for Sakura, who, lost in her memories, sat beneath the cherry trees. She thought of Toshio; how deeply she mourned his death and the loss of their beautiful family home: all gone!

She awoke from her reverie to the sound of Sanford's vehicle landing in the driveway nearby and she rushed for the cottage door, but too late; a hand grabbed her arm and she was cruelly thrown to the floor.

Sanford stood over her, triumphant. "Now who do we have here? An illegal alien, I believe! Do you know that that crime is punishable by death in Britain?"

Sakura spat up at him, catching him full in the face. Sanford instinctively kicked her as she lay beneath him, hitting her in the ribs.

"You coward!" she spat again.

Sanford slowly reached for his hand weapon; he would execute this alien himself!

Just then a child's voice rang out, "Don't hurt my Mummy!" It was Grace, who had heard the mental SOS of her mother.

She was joined by Akemi and Akiyoshi. Each of them in unison repeated over and over the words of Grace; "Don't hurt my Mummy!"

It seemed to Sanford that the words echoed within his skull and resonated through his whole being. Vainly he attempted to raise the weapon, his finger frozen on the grip, he couldn't think at all; just the words drummed over and over again through his skull.

Then, suddenly, he dropped like a fallen tree. The watcher lowered his weapon; Sanford had been top on his list of 'targets of opportunity'.

The Angel Network gratefully retrieved the flying vehicle; it would no doubt be put to a good use. The body of Sanford was too good a propaganda weapon to discard. Within twelve hours, his corpse hung by a noose from the front entrance of the Bee Hive where the invited Press Corps from all over the Euro Zone recorded the sad demise of the second most prominent man in England. The placard that hung from his neck read, "End Emergency Powers Now!"

None of this symbolism escaped Ian McGregor. He knew that the angels were tearing him down piece by piece. His power structure was being dismantled brick by brick; and there was nothing that he could do to prevent it except by an appeal to the Armed Forces. Reluctantly he made the call.

Chapter Fifteen: Pigeons Come Home to Roost

The meeting was held in the GHQ Command conference room. Around the table sat the Service Chiefs, with their Aides in a second circle behind. Manual notes as well as automatic recording of the meeting were taken; nothing was to be left to chance. Ian McGregor sat at one end of the table and Field Marshall David Miller faced him from the other end. Next to him sat General Harvey on his right, Air Chief Marshall Blackwood, and down the table in descending seniority the members of the Joint Chiefs of Staff.

The venue had been deliberately chosen to underline the change of power. McGregor would have preferred to hold the meeting in the Beehive and in fact he requested as much.

To his astonishment, the aide of General Harvey spoke to him in a peremptory tone, "You asked for the meeting, we decide the venue!" Humiliated, McGregor meekly agreed.

GHQ Southern Command is an ancient military academy, where previously the cream of the British Army officer corps was trained. It was formerly known as Sandhurst Military Officers Training Academy. Though much dilapidated, the building still resonated to the sounds of heroes, past and present, who had laid down their lives for their country. Their ghosts still walked the halls, it was said. The establishment reeked with tradition, it was everywhere you turned.

The meeting was being held in the former senior officers' conference room. The walls were panelled in dark British oak and the floor was also of highly polished hardwood, the dark rich colour of the woods a testimony to the unique history and traditions of the establishment.

McGregor was acutely aware that he had entered the power centre of the British Armed Forces, and perhaps for the first time in a long, long while, he felt intimidated. His body language showed as much as he constantly fingered the buttons of his coat.

Field Marshall Miller opened the meeting, addressing McGregor in a similar vein to that of General Harvey's Aide, "You asked for the meeting, now what is on your mind?"

McGregor replied, "Well as you know, we have been facing some difficulties, the scale of which has gone beyond that of a police action which we are well able to…"

Miller interrupted him testily, "Cut to the chase, man, we are well aware of what has been going on, not only now, but ever since you seized power!"

McGregor was definitely not used to being spoken to in this way, he could feel himself reddening, first signs of losing control. No, he must keep it together, much as he detested these buffoons, he needed them and their 'Dad's Army'!

McGregor summoned his confidence and spoke firmly, looking at each of the senior officers as he spoke, "Wrong! A State of Emergency was declared and we acted in defence of the realm to establish law and order; which you have to agree we did do until only a month ago. We consider this a temporary setback and we shall put down this rebellion quickly. It will be faster with your assistance of course, but we shall prevail!" His voice ended on a higher note, not a bad speech if he said so himself.

Miller clapped sardonically, then continued in an acidic tone; "Do you remember General Spencer? Also, do you recall Admiral of the Fleet Foster? And, what of Air Chief Commodore Graves? They were a few of my friends that used to sit at this table. Where are they now, sir? What crime did they commit, sir? I can tell you some of the answers; we don't know where they are, but you do; we don't know what crime they were accused of, because they never stood before a jury of their peers to answer a single accusation, as you very well know, sir! Now you sit before us to beg for our assistance... let me give you our reply- release these officers immediately! If any harm has come to them, you will be held personally responsible. Next, within two weeks we demand a cessation of the Emergency Powers and a return to the laws of the UK. If you bring any foreign troops to support you, we shall take that as a declaration of war and we shall resist the aggressors! Now go! We have no other words to speak to you. You are an abomination, a shame to the name of Britain. In our name you have oppressed the nation and sold out our sovereignty! You have two weeks to make all necessary arrangements; we shall meanwhile attempt mediation with Angel Network to stop the conflict.

If you try to double-cross us we shall cast our lot in with the Angels. Why are you still here? I said go!" He gestured to his aide to escort McGregor out of the conference room.

The personal aide to the Field Marshall Miller, Lt. Colonel John Ballantyne, also known as Jack Bailey, saw McGregor to the door; and with a smirk on his face, he sent the Prime Minister off with a laconic, "See you later, Mac!" The door closed with a firm click, and Ballantyne returned to the table, smiling easily.

McGregor slunk out of the Command conference room like a whipped dog. Behind him he could hear the muted laughter of the Senior Staff Officers celebrating the tongue lashing of Ian McGregor that was so long overdue.

For him there was no turning back; he knew that his enemies would tear him apart like a pack of hungry dogs. He needed time to gather his forces. Yes, the World Council meeting was on May First. He would lobby his allies, perhaps even the Americans? They were eager to re-enter the world stage; perhaps that old 'Special Relationship' could be reignited? Yes, he felt sure that this would work out just fine!

At least he knew who his enemies were now. He would do them down, indeed, and he'd stitch them up alright, like in the old days in Glasgow! Yes, he'd stitch 'em…

"Does yer mammy have a sewing machine?" he'd ask. "Well, tell her to stitch this!" he'd say, as he slashed their face with the razor. Yes, those were the days! Everybody knew to fear wee Ian McGregor in those days!

Still trembling with his humiliation, McGregor reached for his comm link. He placed an urgent video call to Francois Bernard, his ally and Premier for Life of France.

"Francois, Ian here."

"I know, Ian, this is video remember? You seem dreadfully upset, dear boy, why you are positively twitchy!"

"Indeed I am not, Francois. Well, yes I am upset, but I do not twitch!"

Francois paused for a moment. "Hmmm... well, if you say so. What is the reason for the urgent call, Ian?"

"There has been another development, one which could destabilize the whole alliance. I need to meet with both you and Herschel Schwartz personally to discuss this development... I don't trust a remote conference for this matter, it may not be secure!"

"My dear fellow," Francois replied, "I am sure that an encrypted carrier is perfectly secure, but if you insist, we shall meet... always glad to see you old boy, anytime! Where and when shall we meet? How about my place in the country, tomorrow evening at eight o'clock? You know it's very private. It's also easier for Herschel to come there from Euro Central." So it was agreed.

Chapter Sixteen: The Grand alliance

Francois immediately called Herschel Schwartz, leader of the Euro Zone Parliament and leader of the inner circle comprising of Britain, France and Germany. By mutual agreement the Euro Zone leadership rotated every two years between the three partners.

"Herschel? Francois here. Look, Ian has been on the line. He wants an urgent meet, tomorrow night; he's very upset about something, won't discuss it by video conference either. I agree, he might be becoming paranoiac, but anyway we need to meet with him to assess his state. Yes, he is under a lot of pressure, as we all are these days. But with the World Council coming up in just over a week, we need him to be under self-control, so I guess that we have to help him sort out his issues! Why don't we meet earlier, say seven o'clock? The meeting is to be at my place. I might even spring for a spot of early dinner!" It was agreed.

Herschel was a man of few words, a contrast to the flamboyant French Premier, who loved to babble on about seemingly inconsequential matters and filled every conversation with dreadful Anglicized idiom, mostly of the late twentieth century. Herschel was a cold person, nicknamed 'The Iceman' by friend and foe alike. He had a reputation for being logical and calculating. His office was also his residence; it was clinically modernistic, minimalist you might even say. In contrast to his UK partner, Herschel preferred to live where he was surrounded by nature, so the ultra-modern building that housed his office looked out upon parkland and deciduous forest. In fact, he had cleared a swathe of a national park, just so that his personal monorail could access his office, while giving him an uninterrupted view over the treetops as far as the distant Alps.

Herschel was not a calm, clinical person; that was merely a reflex cultivated over many years. As a child he had been delicate in his health, and, as so often was the case, he was bullied by his schoolmates. After one particularly bad bullying event, something snapped inside, and the timid, retiring boy retaliated with dreadful anger. Typically, Herschel calculated his moment carefully; he observed the larger boy's habits, he noted his weaknesses and then he struck.

The boy was apt to cycle down from the school yard to the valley below without wearing his helmet; it was an act of bravado, of flouting authority; one which he was to regret for the rest of his life.

As he reached the crest of the hill, he realized to his horror that his brakes had been sabotaged and his cycle plunged down the tree-lined road, heading for the first of several very steep bends. As Herschel had expected, the boy made it past the first bend but he wouldn't make the next.

As he approached the bend, he looked up to see Herschel standing by the corner, waving and smiling to him as his bike careered off the edge of the road and he became airborne through the fir trees. There was a great sound of snapping branches and just one scream, and then all was silent.

Herschel decided that someone ought to go for help. He sauntered back up the long hill, pausing occasionally to admire the view over the valley and listened to the sounds of the woodpeckers as they worked on the trunks of the fir trees. The boy was eventually found in a tangle of broken branches forty metres below the point that he had left the road. He had a broken collarbone, and his left lung was collapsed owing to the pine branch that had impaled him when he landed. After this no one came near Herschel again.

Herschel sipped his glass of chilled Eiswein, which some call Ice Wine. It seemed to calm him and enabled him to analyse situations almost in an abstract way.

Herschel loved all things German. He particularly liked to sip this dessert wine, which was produced in the Rhineland vineries from grapes that had been frozen while still on the vine. Only the water in the grapes froze, but not the sugars and other dissolved solids, which resulted in a more concentrated, very sweet wine. Herschel loved the sweet, rather acidic taste of this native clear white wine. Because the process produced very small quantities of wine, it was very expensive; but that was of no concern to Herschel, who drank it with every meal and afterwards also.

Behind his back he was called the Ice Man or Eismann in German. This largely came from his detached demeanour, but the origin of the nickname came from the play by Eugene O'Neill called 'The Ice Man Cometh'. It so amused Herschel that it became somewhat of an obsession for a while, as he set about obtaining copies of the play in every media format available; he purchased, as well, the original manuscript from a museum at great expense. As a result, the nickname 'Eismann' stuck to him.

Herschel's love of all things German led him to hate the immigration of Turks and East Europeans who had flooded into Germany over the past one hundred years. Therefore, for him to ally himself with the extremists, so-called neo-Nazi groups, was like a marriage made in heaven.

Under Herschel's leadership the right wing neo-Nazi party gained credibility and respectability. Like Adolf Hitler long ago, he forged a strong partnership with the captains of industry. Germany needed labour, cheap labour in particular; the immigrants from Turkey and East European Countries were an easy target for his propaganda.

Several new laws were passed to isolate these communities, including one that made it a punishable offence to practice any of the world's major religions in Germany, on the grounds that it was culturally offensive and un-German to practice any religion other than Christianity. This was of course a pretext to facilitate the enslavement of immigrants for industrial labour.

Herschel also arranged trade with the Russian Federation. Under the treaty, Germany supplied cheap energy and Russia would send indentured labour to work in Germany's booming economy. It sounded like a lifeline to the unemployed masses of Russians, but in fact it turned out to be nothing but slavery when the employers did not honour the terms of the indenture contracts.

No one could be a greater contrast to Herschel than his partner, Francois Bernard. Francois was from ancient French aristocracy. His name meant 'brave as a bear', but Francois gave every indication of being a dilettante; nothing could be further from the truth. Behind the mask of a clown, cold steel eyes looked out upon the world. The light-hearted banter that characterized his conversations concealed a deadly serious purpose.

Francois was dedicated to restoration of the greatness of France. The French Statesman, President Charles de Gaulle once said, "For glory gives herself only to those who have always dreamed of her." And this was the dream of Francois Bernard; that France would one day take her rightful place as a centre of culture and industry.

He championed the right of the ancient nobility and upper classes to exercise an enlightened feudalism in order to achieve his ultimate goal. Like McGregor, he covertly instigated civil unrest until the tottering moderate government finally abdicated to the will of the right wing, under Bernard's leadership.

Bernard portrayed himself as the consummate patriotic Frenchman and Europhile. For this reason he wooed the far right elements of French politics, supporting their propaganda against the immigrants from North Africa who were flooding into a prospering Europe. But instead of deporting the immigrants and illegal aliens, it was his brainchild to place them into 'centres of industry', which in actual fact were nothing more than slave labour camps.

His 'enlightened policy' was to exert a feudal control over a specific portion of the population, making them productive, so that France might prosper in the new alliance that came to be called the Euro Zone. That he was a major shareholder in many of these corporations which employed the immigrant slaves, was a fact carefully screened from the annual reports of the corporations; he employed proxy companies and individuals to cover his profiteering.

In fact, as more power fell into his hands, he was able to exercise more control over the media and the justice system. Like McGregor, he contrived to create a destabilized society that welcomed his Party with all of its extremism.

Finally, he declared a suspension of the Constitution and imposed Martial Law throughout the country. Like McGregor's Defenders, his right wing extremists exercised total right of search and detention without trial and, in particular, he applied surveillance over the whole population, which he required to wear visible RFID tags at all times. Thus Francois Bernard became absolute ruler over a kingdom of slaves; those who were nominally free, but controlled, and those were confined and severely controlled.

Francois Bernard, never one to do things in less than opulent style, had acquired a luxury hotel resort which was a former chateau of the nobility. Situated at Boutigny-sur-Essonne, which is less than an hour from Paris Central and not far from the Royal district of Fontainebleau, the former hotel and golf resort is framed by a nearby forest and formal gardens; it is a castle fit for the grand aspirations of France's Premier for Life. Within the castle, the decor was completely restored to that of the Louis XIV period.

This grand home was to be the rendezvous for the soiree to be attended by the Chancellor Protector of Germany and Leader of the Euro Zone, Herschel Schwartz, and the Prime Minister of Britain, The Right Honourable Ian McGregor. As privately arranged, Herschel arrived earlier for a brief dinner at seven o'clock with Francois Bernard so that they might prepare for Ian's arrival at eight o'clock that evening. Characteristically, Herschel eschewed the formal ground car limousine journey from Paris Central station in favour of a private jet, which touched down in the grounds of the chateau and within walking distance of the entrance.

Francois greeted Herschel warmly at the door with much affectation and conducted him through the opulence of the former reception area of the hotel; to Francois' mind he had removed a desecration to this home of the nobility and restored it to its former grandeur.

They entered a large reception room where Francois had prepared a dinner for the two of them. The table was big enough to seat twenty people, but they sat facing each other at one end. The waiters carried in a selection of dishes that Francois had made especially for the tastes of his German guest, and the dishes were set out buffet style. There was Schweinshaxe or knuckle of pork, served with sauerkraut and dumplings; Schweinsbraten pork roast; Veal schnitzel served with mushrooms and peppers; Weiswurst, which is a white veal and pork sausage; Obatzda camembert cheese, served with rye bread; some cuts of venison and rabbit accompanied by dumplings; and, of, course, chilled Bavarian beer to wash down these Bavarian delicacies; truly a feast for a king!

"Truly Francois, you have excelled yourself this time!" Herschel exclaimed when he saw the feast. "I could never do justice to this feast!"

"We will save some cold cuts for Ian, perhaps." Francois replied.

The men served themselves and sat down to eat. Francois picked at his choices; the German food was not very much to his liking. Herschel wolfed his down and returned to the buffet several times to refill his plate. Eventually, he was sated and they retired to a drawing room to take brandy and cigars.

"Now, what is on the agenda for the meeting?" Herschel enquired, as he exhaled clouds of blue aromatic smoke.

"To tell you the truth, I've related all that the dear boy said on our video call; we shall have to await his arrival for more details. No, what I wanted to discuss is his general situation. Do you think that he can take the pressure, to put it bluntly?"

Herschel considered for a moment, never being one to rush in, he chose his words carefully. "I'm sure that the Sanford affair must upset him, but since when did the loss of a lackey upset us Olympians?"

"Yes, I agree," Francois replied, "But these other attacks are surely getting him down... I've heard that he is practically a hermit now. He has not left the Bee Hive for a week, according to my informants."

Herschel noted the slip; so Francois did not trust his own partners these days; spying on them? "OK, let's observe him in the meeting."

Chapter Seventeen: Frank Admissions

Ian McGregor arrived with his customary lateness, his private jet landed next to Herschel's and he walked over to the chateau, where Francois and Herschel waited to meet him at the door.

After the usual pleasantries, they made their way into the drawing room where they filled their glasses and toasted each other before settling down in the rather uncomfortable period chairs that Francois affected to like.

Without wasting time on small talk, Ian McGregor got straight to the point. "I am afraid that we are facing a coup. We have been given two weeks to surrender the Emergency Powers or the Armed Forces will take over! At this point I am unaware whether the rebellion has spread to the rest of the Euro Zone, but it must be a distinct possibility." He then proceeded to relate the events leading up to the Sandhurst meeting, and the substance of the ultimatum delivered to him by Field Marshall Miller and the Joint Chiefs of Staff; however he glossed over his personal humiliation.

The room fell silent; you could have heard a pin drop! The Euro Zone partners thought about this amazing disclosure, it was not what they had expected; perhaps a whining appeal for help, but not this!

"This is catastrophic!" exclaimed Francois. "If this rebellion has spread to Europe, everything that we have built together will be destroyed, incredible!"

Herschel raised his hand. "This calls for cool heads, my friend! Now, let us analyse this ultimatum; they have threatened to support the terrorist group, the Angel Network, if we do not comply with their demands within a two week window of time; correct?" Ian McGregor nodded silently.

"They have also made certain demands, such as the lifting of the emergency powers decree and the release of certain senior officers, n'est pas?" interrupted Francois.

"Yes," Herschel continued, "but let us not panic! We mustn't forget that the military have given you two more weeks to resolve the issue; that tells me three things—first, that they are comfortable with the status quo for the time being and, secondly, we have an opportunity to escalate our response by calling upon our Euro Zone partners and our would-be allies, the Americans, at the forthcoming World Council!"

"Surely, faced with overwhelming force they would be forced to back down and you can pick them off one by one later, at your leisure. Thirdly, I don't believe that there is a unified conspiracy across the Euro Zone or we would have heard of it through our sources. What I propose is that we placate them with the release of these senior officers, they are alive, right?"

McGregor answered with a nod of his head. Herschel moved to sum up. "Good, that makes it easier. So are we agreed; we release the three officers and we keep them guessing about the lifting of the Emergency until after the first of

May? Then we will move quickly to crush them, using the combined forces of the Euro Zone! Let's schedule some War Games exercises in the North Sea, which should keep them preoccupied meanwhile and allow us to reposition our forces."

It was a plan! They all felt that they were firmly in control again and the axis of their partnership, although a bit wobbly, was now realigned and they would soon be back in top gear. There was just the irritation of the local resistance efforts to destabilize the Euro Zone, but that would soon be dealt with.

At that very moment, a team of saboteurs was crossing the lawns of the chateau. Having penetrated the alarm systems using Dr Stewart's descanner, the commandos silently killed the outer perimeter guards and then proceeded just as silently to take out the inner ring of security. All resistance having been neutralized for the time being, they placed explosive charges about the chateau and the vehicles of the visiting heads of state.

The said visitors and their host sat in the drawing room comfortably swapping anecdotes about their successes in the establishment of their regimes. A few similarities emerged and they congratulated themselves upon their acumen.

Then all three comm. links rang together. Each bore a single text message from an anonymous source; "BOOM!"

This was followed by a series of explosions that rocked the walls of the chateau and the floor beneath their feet shook. Immediately, they rushed for the exit, but the scene that met their eyes defied belief; through the clouds of black dust swirling in the reception area they could see that beyond, where the front door used to be there was now a gap; not a hole, a gap. The entire front of the chateau was gone; just a pile of broken masonry and roof tiles!

Over the lawn, two heaps of mangled metal marked the place where the two private jets had parked. Dead bodies of servants and soldiers lay scattered about the chateau grounds and they seemed to be the only survivors!

"Guess we walk home, eh, Herschel?" McGregor asked laconically.

Just then, Herschel received another anonymous text message. "Don't go home, you need a hotel!" For the first time in a long, long while, he lost his cool; he howled with grief and frustration, that they would do this to him, and to his beautiful home?

Francois, meanwhile, was beside himself; he was totally devastated. How did they penetrate his screen of scanners? How did they get past his elite guards, all of them black belts in martial arts? His mind reeled; he was going to have a nervous breakdown, and proceeded to do so.

Chapter Eighteen: Homecomings

The next morning, Ian McGregor wearily exited the Superliner, now flanked by a squad of armed Defenders. Security was at a maximum, and cordons had been erected wherever possible. It was such a come-down to have to return home like a common man.

Safely penned in behind the security barriers, foreign tourists took a rare image opportunity and immediately transmitted the captured images off to their home countries before the Defenders could react by confiscating the comm. links. Thus the whole world instantly saw the pictures of the uncharacteristically dishevelled Prime Minister of Great Britain arriving at London Metropolis Central station; weariness lined his face and it was unmistakable that he appeared to be nervously glancing all about him as the phalanx of Defenders escorted him to a waiting limousine on the platform of the station.

Herschel Schwartz was also spotted by some intrepid newshounds at Euro Zone Central, and it was also remarked upon that the normally dapper German High Chancellor looked quite the worse for wear. He was also whisked away by limousine to an unknown location.

Soon, both sets of photographs were circulating about the Web, beyond the reach of the Censors, who were frankly caught off guard. Journalists also flocked to the chateau at Boutigny-sur-Essonne where explosions had been heard during the night before. They interviewed some locals in the village nearby, but they were prevented from getting within sight of the Chateau by a ring of heavily armed security guards who motioned them away if they attempted to converse. The locals did report, however, that a medivac had arrived in the night, shortly after the series of explosions, and departed again shortly thereafter. No one had any more information, but the newshounds were on the scent now and it was quickly established that a medivac rotor vehicle had arrived last night in Paris Central at the hospital normally reserved for VIP officials, and a patient had disembarked. Further enquiries revealed that it was indeed the Premier, Francois Bernard, that had been admitted, but the nature of his injuries was not disclosed. A hospital statement was issued subsequently which stated that, as the result of a gas explosion at the Chateau, the Premier had been admitted for observation. The statement also said that his personal physician was attending and he expected to discharge the Premier shortly and his admittance was only a precaution.

In actual fact, at the time that the statement was being given to the press, Francois Bernard was strapped to a gurney in the psych ward and he was treated with psychotropic drugs for the next twelve hours until he became calmer and lucid enough to convince the Medical Supervisor that he was not a danger to himself or anyone else. He was immediately given a discharge, and he left by a private jet from the roof of the hospital in order to avoid the crowds who were thronging the ground floor of the hospital, waiting for a sight of him.

There were too may coincidences for the media to ignore the obvious; both McGregor and Schwartz had returned from a meeting in Paris; both looking weary and dishevelled; Premier Bernard's chateau had clearly been bombed and he was undergoing medical treatment. Putting the pieces of the puzzle wasn't too hard; this was a deliberate strike against the triumvirate of Euro Zone, and even an idiot could see that this had to be linked to the escalating series of attacks that were occurring in Germany, France and Britain. Press statements being put out by the respective government were almost the same, word for word; this was a cover up at the highest level and public confidence was shaken.

Shortly after the official French Government statement, the following was posted on the Web;

"The Free French Resistance was responsible for the bombing last evening at the Chateau Boutigny-sur-Essonne. We reject the authority of the Regime led by Francois Bernard, which is an illegitimate government that enslaves free men for his personal profit. We also condemn the illegal annexation of the North African Territories and we call upon Frenchmen everywhere to rise up and overthrow these oppressors. We shall escalate our military strikes until we bring these tyrants to their knees; the guilty shall by no means escape!"

In view of Bernard's delicate mental state, the hospital's psychiatric specialist and Bernard's personal aides agreed that the Free French Resistance (FFR) statement should be kept from Bernard until he had recovered his composure. The printed text was, however, smuggled into his room by a FFR sympathizer and it was almost the first thing that he saw when he opened his eyes. The resulting screams brought the doctors running to his bedside; more drugs were immediately administered. This was the true reason for the Premier's prolonged stay in the hospital.

Lt. Colonel John Ballantyne, in his persona as Jack Bailey, dismounted the Superliner at London Metropolis shortly after the Prime Minister. In contrast to the PM's, his demeanour was cheerful and he walked with a spring in his step. The members of his team of eight commandos also left the Maglev train, but individually; they all passed through the barriers without setting off the suspicion of the Defenders on duty because of their military IDs and the descanners that they carried, which neutralized the metal detectors.

Outside the station, Jack Bailey boarded a ground car stretch limousine that awaited him at the kerbside. His team also boarded a second stretch limousine and the two vehicles took off in a leisurely drive westward out of London Metropolis Central.

Jack sat back in the comfortable seats of the limousine and accepted the proffered Scotch and ice from the elderly gentleman who sat across from him. Silently, they observed the flow of ground cars about the station precincts; so many people in a hurry to get somewhere!

"I take it that the trip went well, John?" the elderly gentleman asked solicitously.

"Yes," John Ballantyne replied, "all went exactly to plan; the objective was achieved with no casualties on our side at all, Field Marshall."

Chapter Nineteen: A Walk in the Fields

Springtime in Somerset is a time of green pastures and flowers putting forth their show in every hedge, field and wood; a splash of colour here, a swathe of blue there; a time of new beginnings.

On a fine spring morning, in the last week of April, the warmth of the sun had dried off the morning mist, and the Stewart family decided to go for a walk. Sakura and Jim headed off along the valley where the streambed gushed with pure runoff from the Mendip Hills. Along the stream the willows were coming to bloom and the catkins hung from the branches, slightly swaying in the gentle breeze. Wild garlic flowers bloomed with their spiky white flowers on long stems and the air was filled with the heady scent of garlic in the air.

Down the path, as they walked, Jim decided to broach a question. "You never told me how you reached England and how you managed to get into that private pod on the Exeter Express."

Sakura laughed, "And I thought that women were the curious ones! But it's a fair question, I suppose, and you do deserve to know as much as I can tell you."

"Well, we'll begin in Kyoto; after the raid by the E.A.R. under General Chi, we fled through a tunnel to a safe house that my father and mother had organized for just such an emergency as this. He had expected it and he had arranged that we would be sheltered by the Underground Movement of Japan; Asuka and Ren too, because they were named in the laboratory files. We had to explain to the leader of the Japanese Underground all about the KP and what we believed it could do for the world. He understood the implications. He said that he would look into evacuating us to the West where it was thought that we would be safer than in the E.A.R. We now know that he made contact with Jack Bailey through their contacts and we waited in Kyoto while the Resistance worldwide negotiated together."

"It took nearly a year, but eventually we were ready to go. Grace and I went first, and it was remarkably simple; we just boarded a stratosjet from New Tokyo to Paris Central, under an assumed identity for me and Grace. We didn't have any difficulty in switching identities once we reached Paris, so it would be difficult to trace us from Kyoto to London Central. We simply changed our documents over and lined up to receive visas for a thirty-day visit as tourists; it was that easy! Once we reached London, we were passed information by an agent of the Angels that told us where we were to join you in your pod. Using her powers of suggestion, Grace managed to convince the conductor that we were your family and that you would be joining us shortly, which you did. It was thought too risky to try the same procedure again for the others, so they had to come through different portals into Euro Zone. It was not expected that you would have to rescue Ren and Akemi from Turkey but, as you see, everything turned out alright in the end!"

145

"Well that's an understatement, if ever I heard one!" Jim replied with a laugh.

They sat quietly by the stream, enjoying the warm sun on their faces and the sounds of the birds in the wood nearby. Slowly, hesistantly, their hands touched and shyly Sakura accepted Jim's hand in hers.

"It was meant to be," she whispered, and they kissed.

Just then Grace came bounding out of the willows, where no doubt she had been spying on them. They laughed, a little embarrassed at first, but then it was alright again, as Grace took both of their hands in hers and said, "Daddy, why don't you show us the English spring flowers?" They walked on together, as a threesome united finally.

They climbed up into the woods which grew nearby. There was a narrow path which wound its way between the trees.

"Come," said Jim, "I'll show you a magic carpet, Grace!"

"Really, oh! I must see it at once!" the little girl shouted with excitement. Jim and Sakura followed on behind talking quietly, but Grace ran ahead, impatient to see the magic carpet of the woods. After a short while, the path dipped into a grassy valley, and there it was; the magic carpet, as Jim had promised. A great carpet of bluebells, as far as you could see in the wood. Every clearing had a swathe of the beautiful, bright blue flowers, and here and there, peeping out from the shaded places; white primroses, white bells of snowdrops, and even here and there, secreted in old oak tree stumps, the occasional glory of purple orchids could be seen, and the shy wood anemone peeped out from behind a bush here and there.

"Oh, Daddy! It really is a magic carpet, and this is a magic wood!" the little girl cried.

"See," said Jim with a smile, "this is a magic wood, and Somerset is a magic land and it's full of magical people, Aaaah!" He finished with a fierce expression and a roar, and the delighted Grace ran off screaming with pleasure. It was good to be able to do the simple things; to take time out to be normal people for a while.

Soon it was time to go back to the farm. They decided to take the long way back over the fields where the sheep roamed with their new lambs or grazed contentedly on the pastures. Jim pointed out to Grace some of the flowers of the field; the moon daisies, white with yellow hearts, that grew on the verges of the field; these Grace gathered in bunches so that she could weave chains of flowers back at the farm; then the creamy white of the campion, growing here and there in the meadow and its cousin, the red campion, which preferred the sheltered edge of the wood or hedgerows.

"Perhaps tomorrow, if the weather is not too wet, we could explore the caves of Priddy." Jim suggested.

"But would it matter if it rained, if we were inside?" Sakura enquired.

"Oh, rather," answered Jim. "You see the rock here is mostly limestone overlaid with chalk, so when it rains the water just soaks through into the water reservoirs, the underground streams start to flow and the basins fill up. Sometimes this can happen very quickly and people can get cut off from the escape route. Some have even drowned in some of these caves."

"There are very extensive cave systems just to the west of here at Wookey Hole and Cheddar Gorge; people come from all over the world just to see the amazing formations, which are called stalagmites and stalactites. They are quite famous!" Grace curiously wanted to know what are stalagmites and stalactites, so Jim explained. "The water flows through the limestone rock. As it drips from the roof to the floor of the water chamber, trace deposits of calcium are deposited on the roof until they form a tiny column of limestone. The water drips from the tiny column and starts the same process all over again from the floor. This time the ground column grows up toward the roof. One day the two columns will touch each other and set hard as concrete to form a single column. When I was little, it was explained to me like this; stalactites hang down from the roof, so they hang on 'tight'; stalagmites grow up towards the stalactites on the roof, so they 'might' reach the roof. We will see this for ourselves when we go exploring. The other children can come too; we'll make a day of it, and perhaps we could have a picnic!"

"Oh, yes, Jim!" Sakura hugged Jim happily, all reserve melted away now. "It has been so long since we had a picnic, hasn't it Grace?" The little one bubbled with glee and couldn't wait to get back to the farm to share her news with Akiyoshi and Akemi.

When they reached the farm, everyone was sitting together playing some games that John had set up on an ancient computer that Akiyoshi had unearthed in a storage room. The games were quite primitive; only simple three-dimensional virtual reality, of course, but the graphics were interesting in a quaint sort of way.

The game that they were engaged in now was a sort of competitive team game and Jim and Sakura couldn't help but notice that the adult pairings seemed relaxed and comfortable together; Bill with Asuka and John with Ren. There was something in the air alright.

"Must be spring fever," Jim whispered in Sakura's ear, at which she dissolved into a fit of giggles; but the players played on, oblivious to everything outside of the game environment and their partners.

Soon, it was lunchtime and the ladies headed off to the kitchen to prepare some food. It had been agreed that they would alternate cuisines; today it was to be Japanese style and the trio promised that it would be as authentic as they could make it. Having been forewarned, Jim had made an excursion down to Plymouth at first light, with a long shopping list, to find the freshest fish available at the quayside and vegetables that a farmer friend grew organically on his farm near the coast.

In the fishing port, the small boats still resembled the boats that generations of Cornish fishermen had sailed in the dangerous coastal waters. Today he was fortunate because he came early and there were mackerel, herring, mullet, clams; the mullet had just been landed by a local fisherman, so Jim took basket loads for his hungry crowd. On the farm he found potatoes, carrots, beans, mustard greens, onions and tomatoes; not all terribly authentic Japanese fare, but they would have to do; he couldn't risk a trip to a large city yet.

In a local store, to his great surprise, he found a Japanese food section; mostly dried foods and packets of powdered soups, but he was sure that the ladies would more than manage to improve upon the men's last effort!

Although Kyoto was inland and surrounded by mountains, the natives loved fish of all kinds, and many of the local recipes included fish and of course rice or tofu. The latter was hard for Jim to find in the small store in Plymouth, but he was able to buy enough for one meal at least.

Dried seaweed, all kinds of fish and clams are all popular ingredients in Japanese cooking, so the mullet and clams were all put to good use. Also, the enterprising ladies were able to make tasty fishcakes from the mackerel that Jim had bought. They were also able to add some ingredients – the packet of dried Miso soup – to give the meal the ring of authenticity of a Japanese-style meal. Some dried seaweed received some kitchen magic also, and it was served with the organic vegetables from the farm. Soy sauce spiced with wasabi paste and authentic Japanese rice all combined to make a very passable Japanese meal, which they ate with chopsticks that Jim had also found in the Supermarket.

The quantity that they had made was more than enough for the three adults and three children, so they preserved the excess by freezing what they could for next time. It was an idyllic interlude and they all determined to make the most of it while it lasted.

Chapter Twenty: Truth or Consequences

The rotor vehicle carrying the insignia of the Defenders swooped down over the town of Sandhurst, Berkshire and made a clumsy landing in the parade ground of the GHQ, formerly known as the Royal Military Academy, Sandhurst.

The side door opened and three men were unceremoniously pushed out of the door. They staggered and fell in the dust. The Defenders' vehicle roared away in a storm of dust with both turbos on full power.

As the three men slowly got to their feet, their eyes squinted against the unaccustomed power of the daylight. The armed guards who surrounded the three elderly men kept them covered with levelled laser rifles.

A sergeant-at-arms strode up to the encircled men. He looked at them carefully; they were dressed in grey dungarees and work boots, and from the top of their heads to their boots they were filthy. From their eyes, tears ran down their cheeks, leaving streaks in the caked-on dirt on their faces.

The sergeant issued the obligatory challenge: "Sirs, please identify yourselves!" But the shock of seeing the state of these elderly men softened his tone somewhat. He repeated the challenge because the men had made no response whatsoever. "Sirs, please identify yourselves!"

The nearest of the three straightened himself with an effort, raised his head and pulled his shoulders back in the semblance of a military posture of attention, though he swayed as he stared into the sergeant's eyes, then he spoke out with a clear voice.

"Sir, I am General Sir Irving Spencer. These other gentlemen are Admiral of the Fleet David Foster, Air Chief Marshall Gerald Graves, and if you please, we would like a drink of water and then a shower, sir!"

Field Marshall Miller stood before the window looking out over the Sandhurst parade ground. In his hand he held a whisky glass, which was half full. He turned and spoke.

"Gentlemen, the ground I am looking out over has seen many officers passing out from here, some of them kings, nobles of many realms, most of these officers sacrificed their lives for a cause that they believed in. They did so for love of country, for honour, and because they placed their trust in the integrity of their leadership. But gentlemen, I tell you, every one of them would be proud to shake your hands today!" So saying, the Field Marshal turned to face the trio of liberated Senior Officers, a tear in his eye, and he solemnly raised his glass and toasted the three men who had endured the unjust imprisonment and torture of John Sanford, and did not crack.

The Field Marshall continued, "Gentlemen, you will no doubt be gratified to learn that your tormentor is dead! But we are all the more resolved to finish this fight, to root out this nest of rats and cleanse our land!"

The boardroom erupted with a chorus of "Hear, hear!" and the entire company of senior officers assembled, enthusiastically applauded the trio of heroes.

A little while later, the Field Marshall and Lt.Col. John Ballantyne sat in the Field Marshall's office. It was time to discuss the next steps.

"John," the Field Marshall said," I think that we have to double up our protection of the assets. Sanford is gone but his successor will be appointed soon, and we must assume that he will pick up where Sanford left off in his investigations."

John replied, "Yes, sir, that is in hand, but there is interest from other sources too. We know that the E.A.R. has a top operative here, just arrived in fact, and this man has been leading the manhunt for our trio. Inside sources in Euro Central tell us that Wolf Braun from the Euro Zone Security Department is also getting very close; the Russians are also in the chase, but we don't think that they know exactly what they are chasing!"

"Hmmm, it's going down to the wire, John, we have only a few more days until the activation of stage three. We are ready, aren't we?"

"Yes, sir," John answered. "The Angels will do their part too, and we are coordinating our actions with the foreign groups so that our strikes will be simultaneous. Now what do we do about this order from McGregor that we shall participate in a North Sea War Games event?"

The Field Marshall exploded in laughter. "John, I can give you several reasons that we can give McGregor for why we won't be participating: first, this isn't like organizing a picnic which can be done in a couple of days, so "No! It's impossible"; secondly, he has an ulterior motive in bringing foreign forces within close range, so "No! It's implausible"; and thirdly, our ultimatum to him specifically warned him against bringing foreign troops here and we said that would be taken as a threat, so the answer to his given excuse is, "No! It's improbable!" We aren't taking orders from him anymore. We have our own plans and he has, as expected shown bad faith. Time for another object lesson, eh, John?"

"Indeed, sir, happy to oblige. Air or ground this time?"

"Air, I think, John. So much more dramatic, don't you agree?"

Chen Li and his team of eight investigators walked from the E.A.R. Embassy in London Central and boarded the three ground cars that awaited them at the Embassy Gate. They carried several suitcase sized bags which contained various pieces of weaponry. The last bag to be loaded into the third car contained a mobile GPR, that is Ground Penetrating Radar; Chen Li was leaving nothing to chance, because he had thoroughly researched his target area and knew the geology of the Priddy area.

The cars pulled away in a convoy, making good time on the aerial roads out of London Central;

they were unaware that a blacked-out limousine was unobtrusively tailing them electronically by a tracking device that had been planted on the lead car.

Several blocks behind the limousine, the Angels operatives were simultaneously tracking both cars, having placed trackers on both of them. It was a cat and mouse game, but here the cat was being stalked by a tiger!

The convoy was able to make good time on the Western Parkway and they sped along at one hundred and eighty kilometres per hour with total disregard for the speed limit, trusting in their diplomatic plates to dissuade any traffic cop foolish enough to attempt to stop them.

Both the ground car and the aerial reconnaissance vehicles remained in constant communication with John Ballantyne who monitored the procession from his base at GHQ in Berkshire.

"What do you propose to do when they arrive at Priddy, sir?" the duty officer asked John.

"Well, we will give them enough rope to hang themselves and then we will pull it in tight! Dr Stewart has been advised of the situation and he has agreed to act as bait. We will station men inside the entrapment area for the Stewarts' protection, and then we will draw these assassins in and strike. Hopefully the weather will hold up, but the weather forecast for the Somerset area is not good at all. That's my chief concern, really."

Indeed, as the procession moved further west, more storm clouds appeared, and, by the time that they reached the sleepy city of Wells, Somerset, the sky was full of black clouds and the forecasted storm was imminent. Thunder rolled over the Mendip Hills and lightning flashes lit up the gloomy day. Soon, large raindrops began to fall, a portent of the heavy downpour to come.

In the tailing limousine, a squad of Russian agents sat impatiently waiting for the action to begin. By now they were sure that the Chinese were close to capturing a biological weapon, as their informants had assured them, and the idea of dispossessing the E.A.R. of their prize as well as exacting revenge for the loss of their colleagues was so sweet that they could almost taste it!

They were so intent upon the chase that they failed to observe the aerial vehicle following them all the way from London Central, now visible and then hidden by the low cloud cover.

The E.A.R. ground limousines slowed to negotiate the narrow lanes up to Priddy. Two teams entered the Stewart farm driveway while the others drove up along the lane to a point nearest to the Priddy Caves entrance.

The squad at the farm divided into two teams. One team silently fanned out around the farm buildings searching for lookouts or guard dogs. The place was quiet, eerily quiet. Chen Li felt the hairs on the back of his neck bristle; he knew that he was being watched by unseen eyes, but there was no one to be seen, and from within the cottages there was no sound.

Using his throat mike, he instructed his teams to exercise extreme caution but to proceed with the search. Two cottages were locked, the doors were forced quickly and two men entered to see empty rooms; satisfied that the rooms were vacant, they rejoined Chen Li in front of the central cottage.

He ordered the GPR to be activated. Held in the horizontal position it showed no persons inside the cottages, thermal imaging was also neutral. Chen Li was puzzled; had they been warned? He entered the cottage. It was indeed empty and there were signs of a hasty departure but what was most interesting was the large area of the floor opened to reveal steps going down into a well-lit laboratory.

Chen Li's heart raced; now they would capture the Hokaidas' secret formula. In his excitement, uncharacteristically, Chen Li threw caution to the wind; he ordered all four of his men to go down and investigate whether there was an escape tunnel.

They confirmed that there did seem to be such a tunnel and they could force apart the doors which had sealed it; and from outside the cottage the GPR operator traced the tunnel as going off in the direction of the Priddy Caves. Gotcha! They would catch them between their two squads!

Chen Li ordered the Cave squad to advance inside and as they did so, to look for signs of recent workings; that would show which way the Stewarts would exit. Chen Li was very happy; all of the planning was going to pay off at last!

He walked out of the cottage, oblivious to the shouts of his men as the floor panel silently slid back into position; beneath his feet his men fell like they had been pole-axed as the gas entered through the ceiling vents.

Chen Li heard the sound of tyres on gravel and looked around to see a blacked out limousine slowly advancing toward him. It had to be the Russians! He looked around him. Where were his men? There was no one; he was alone! He turned and ran as fast as he could, now slipping and slithering in the mud as the rain started to pour down.

Chen Li was never much of an athlete, but fear pumped adrenaline through his veins, and he ran that day like an Olympian uphill on the muddy track that led towards the Priddy Circles. Evidently his pursuers lost sight of him in the heavy rain, and he hid himself behind the giant granite slab of one of the standing stones. His heart pumped frantically, his chest heaved and he gasped for air. No sounds about him now, yet still he waited, he would wait until nightfall if necessary; he was too experienced to rush out into the arms of the Russians!

Following the alert given by Jack Bailey, Jim had organized the evacuation with military precision. The women and children went first in the escape pods, which they retrieved by system command, and then the three brothers exited. Their route was to be as before, following the tunnel to the exit in the fields, but this time they could hear sounds coming from the caves.

"Quick! They are trying to catch us in a pincer movement, guys!" John warned. "Those in the lab are toast! But the others don't know the caves as we do. If we can make it to cistern number three, they won't be able to follow us because already the water is rising from this rainstorm and number two will be totally flooded very soon. We'd best get moving, eh?" They all agreed and with torches and ropes in hand, they turned away to follow the narrow aperture that linked the caves.

Jack Bailey's men entered the cave through the main entrance. The heavy wooden door, which was usually padlocked shut, stood open; this confirmed their suspicion that the E.A.R. were trying to come around the back of the Stewart family. Ahead of them they could hear the E.A.R. agents cursing and banging about as they tried to navigate the pathway.

For the first fifty metres there was a ropeway and this made walking quite easy, but after that the rope was deteriorated and presently they came upon a broken end above an elevated rock. They shone their lamps down and sure enough there had been a casualty, or more accurately, a fatality; a Chinese man lay impaled on a stalagmite fully two metres above the floor of the cavern. It was a warning to tread carefully.

The water by now was cascading off the rocks and seeping through the roof at an alarming rate. Cistern number one was already at chest height but number two might be impassable by now because it required special breathing equipment to negotiate that long section. Bailey's squad decided to stay put and make lots of noise so as to drive the Chinese into a natural trap.

Ahead of them, the E.A.R. team had struggled on. Hearing the sounds behind them, they needed no urging forward; if they went back now they would be caught like rats in a trap. They climbed along on the bed of what was now a raging torrent. If not for the ropes linking them they might easily have been swept away. How deep would the water get before it subsided?

With dismay the beams of their flashlights played along the roof of the cistern. No crevices or shafts to climb up to; and what was that on the roof? It was moss! This cistern was going to be their tomb!

Frantically, they clawed at the rocks seeking to progress faster than the rapidly rising waters. The flooding of the cistern took only five minutes, and they didn't make it. It would be weeks before the smell of rotting corpses led search teams to their bodies, deep in cistern number four.

Chen Li needed not to have feared the pursuit of the Russians; they never made it as far as the edge of the Priddy Circles. On the same muddy track that Chen Li had fled by, the bodies of the Russian agents lay face down in the mud, cut down by the expert marksmen of the Angels.

Chen Li checked his belt and holster. Where were his weapons? Oh, no! They must have slipped from him when he was scrambling up the hillside.

He decided to venture a peek over the top of a fallen capstone. Before him, there stood a child, a boy; the boy didn't utter a word. They stood silently looking at each other. The rain continued to pour down. It streamed down the face of the boy, but he gave it no attention.

"This must be the Japanese boy," Chen Li realized, "but the boy looked mostly European." Behind him he heard another faint noise above the howling of the wind and he turned to see two more children, both girls, of the same age as the boy and identical in facial appearance. It was weird; the children just stood there silently looking at him, while the wind howled and the rain poured down in torrents. They began to speak, but he couldn't see their lips moving.

"Why have you come here? You have to go!" The last four words seemed to come at him from all three sides, they repeated again and again, they drummed in his head, becoming louder and louder; he could not think of anything else, except *"You have to go!"*. His mind began to spin. What was happening to him? He reeled and almost fell. His whole world was now reduced to those four words; blood began to trickle down from his scalp, his eyes and his nose; inside his ears he could feel the blood dripping down and in his mouth he could taste blood; his blood.

He screamed. He began to run, anywhere, somewhere else, somewhere downhill, yes, just as far away as he could get away from those children; he had to save himself!

General Chi stood to receive the medical expert who entered his temporary London Embassy office.

"Your Excellency, we have completed our assessment of the chief operative, Mr. Chen Li."

"And what are your findings, Doctor?" the General enquired.

"Well, we found no explanation for the blood which was all over Li's head; no wounds or abrasions of any kind. Our conclusion is that he has been under tremendous psychological stress and the blood resulted from cranial haemorrhages during this period of extreme stress."

The General considered the report for a few moments and then asked, "Doctor, did Chen Li have any coherent words of explanation for his condition?"

"No, sir, he mostly mumbles and laughs to himself! But he kept talking about witches and witchcraft, just that; witches and witchcraft all over Somerset!"

"Thank you, Doctor. Have Chen Li secured for repatriation. We will have him confined in a mental institution in Beijing; he is of no further use to me!"

He watched from his office as a struggling Chen Li was placed in the back of a transport wearing a strait jacket. He would be given drugs to calm him down for the flight home. Such a waste! He was such a good detective too.

But, General Chi reflected, that Kyoto affair could now be safely swept under the carpet and Chen Li's files could be purged of any evidence that might have been prejudicial to Chi; yes, that was one positive outcome out of all this mess. He would also ensure that full responsibility for the deaths of eight operatives in London, as well as the four who died in Kocaali, Turkey would be attributed to Chen Li's bungling and incompetent direction; surely his mental illness was beginning to affect his judgment, even back then. "Yes," he brightened up, "there are several good outcomes after all!"

In two days, the E.A.R. would be participating in the World Council Conference and General Chi had been requested by the Great Leader to oversee the security of the delegation. This was a great honour. Surely his star was still rising; who knew where it might reach?

Minister Chi - yes, he liked the sound of that! He would go to inspect the Conference Forum and he would ascertain that his directives for the security were being implemented. The highest level of screening was required, there had been threats... but Chi was confident that with his counter-measures in place, no one would even attempt to penetrate the cordon of protection and remote sensing scanners.

Chapter Twenty-One: The Scales Fall

On April 29th, a Scranton Jump Jet that had been loaned to the Angels by Jack Bailey warmed its engines in the early morning chill air. The mission had specified an object lesson to Ian McGregor, and what better target again than McGregor's pride and joy, the Bee Hive Building?

The Bee Hive looked for all the world like a honeycomb or a hornets' nest. The latter probably suited it best considering the nature of the occupying government departments. The Prime Minister's office occupied the top floor; the Ministry for Home Affairs took the next nine lower floors; the Minister for Public Security had occupied the Fiftieth floor; and the next twenty lower floors of the building was HQ for the Defenders Brigades, undertaking civilian surveillance and scrutiny of all passport applications and visa requests. From floor twenty nine down to floor twenty it was for the Progress party; then to floor fifteen it was all espionage and counter terrorism; and then the remainder was for day to day police work which had formerly been undertaken by the old Metropolitan Police. In short, the Bee Hive was the very nerve centre of Ian McGregor's regime.

The Scranton's mission was planned for a strike at precisely twelve noon. The jet was fully armed and carried an awesome payload that was to deliver a message from the Joint Chiefs of Staff.

Meanwhile, the Court of St. James had extended an invitation to The Right Honourable Ian McGregor, Prime Minister of Great Britain, to attend an audience with King Charles the Fourth at Buckingham Palace. He was expressly asked to attend at eleven forty five a.m. precisely.

McGregor was in half a mind not to go at all; who did the old fool think he was? Did he imagine that he still had even a vestige of real authority? Everyone knew that he was senile, a clear case of Alzheimer's Syndrome, if ever he saw one! Nevertheless, he decided that he would go through with it. Heaven knows he needed some light relief from the past week's dramas!

As a sign of his disrespect he chose to arrive in an aerial rotor vehicle instead of the limousine normally required by protocol. He would do this on his own terms, he determined!

The Defenders on duty saluted him as he entered the inner quadrangle of the Palace, and McGregor walked briskly under the portico into the Palace where he was met by the Master of the Kings' Household. He was accompanied by the King's Personal Equerry and together they proceeded along the long corridor and up two flights of stairs to the Audience Room. McGregor had not visited for a while, being preoccupied with more important matters of State, but the ornate furnishings and walls covered with the finest silk never ceased to amaze and impress him. The carpets of finest English Axminster wool and the silk wall tapestries hanging from ceiling to floor were also most impressive, were it not for the terrible pervading smell of damp throughout the Palace.

He was conducted into the Audience Room, where His Britannic Majesty sat alone, a Bible by his side on a low table.

The King greeted him with a most unusual salutation; "Are you a man of The Book, Mr. Prime Minister?"

"Well, no, Your Majesty," McGregor replied with a sigh. This was not going to be much fun after all!

The King continued as if he had missed the sigh, "Oh, yes, I read it every day, never miss a day, you know. Take today's reading for instance; it was taken from Second Chronicles 22;11-12. I'll read it for you, you may find it interesting."

"Verse 11: But Jehoshabeath, the daughter of the king, took Joash the son of Ahaziah, and stole him from among the king's sons that were slain, and put him and his nurse in a bedchamber. So Jehoshabeath, the daughter of king Jehoram, the wife of Jehoiada the priest, (for she was the sister of Ahaziah,) hid him from Athaliah, so that she slew him not."

"Verse 12: And he was with them hid in the house of God six years; and Athaliah reigned over the land."

"See, this Joash was the last surviving true heir of the direct line of the King, and this Athaliah was a wicked Queen, you know; she actually murdered all of the king's family so that she could reign herself. Rather as you did, Mr McGregor, when you murdered my son and all of the heirs to the throne; or so you thought! But Divine Providence hid a sole heir from your hands and we have kept him safe all of these years, right under your nose, Mr Prime Minister!"

McGregor reeled at the revelation coming from the King. Could this be the same bumbling old man who had shuffled his way into the Progress Party State Banquets? He looked up and saw the transformation as the King raised his head up; gone was the stoop and the hunched shoulders, gone was the trembling voice; the face which was lined with grief yet bore a regal dignity that McGregor had never witnessed; and the eyes... they burned with an intense bright blue, they seemed to look straight through him and into his soul!

"Please come in!" the King said. From a side door a young man entered. He was almost two metres tall and he too had the intense blue eyes of the old King. "Allow me to introduce my Grandson, Prince Arthur, and heir to the throne of Britain!"

"But, but, how, how was this done?" stammered McGregor in a flat panic. "And you, you are so changed, what has happened to you, your Majesty?"

The King answered him with open loathing in his voice, "You undeserving reptile! You were dosing me with drugs; you tried to poison me in my own household! But eventually we caught your agent and he was fed with his own poison! Since then, the Angels have been watching over me and they have restored me, thanks to a new

168

treatment; so my 'youth is renewed like the eagle' as the Good Book says. You really ought to read it, while you still have the time," he concluded as an aside. "Now McGregor, I have laid on a show for you, just for your benefit. Come with me to the balcony. We shall watch it together!"

As a lamb, McGregor followed the King to the balcony which gave onto a view down The Mall. At the other end of The Mall, where formerly Whitehall Street had met Trafalgar Square and where the ancient monument to a British hero, Nelson, had stood, the hideous Bee Hive building now dominated the view.

It was twelve noon exactly. A flight of military jets flew past the Palace at a low altitude. As they passed by, they dipped their wings in salute to the King. A lone jet circled the Bee Hive, like a bird of prey selecting its target. It was a Scranton. Suddenly McGregor had a sense of foreboding, and nausea in the pit of his stomach.

"No, no, no! Not that, please not that!" he cried; he tried to turn away, but a pair of muscular young hands pinned his arms to his side and the King's hand on his chin forced him to watch.

The Scranton fired the first missile directly at the Sixtieth floor. It was a multi warhead rocket designed for maximum destruction of tanks; the flimsy construction of the Beehive was no match for it.

Floor after floor was systematically destroyed until all of the armaments were used up. A second plane joined the demolition, then a third, and a fourth, and they kept coming!

Finally all that was remaining of the pride of the Progress Party HQ and the site of McGregor's seat of power was totally destroyed. For a long moment, the building tottered as if somehow it might find its balance and stand again, but then the frame of the structure began to tilt and twist and it collapsed upon itself. Finally it dropped upon its own ruin; a heap of broken dreams, twenty stories high!

McGregor howled in anguish and would have dropped to his knees were it not for the strong hands which gripped him.

"Mr McGregor, I have some instructions for you; get control of yourself!" the King ordered. He continued, "Now, I am your monarch, and this is what you are going to do. At the World Council Conference on May the First, you will make two announcements. First, you will announce the lifting of the Emergency Powers Act and disbanding of the Defenders. Second, you will announce the dissolution of the Progress party with all of its associations, foreign and domestic. Have I made myself crystal clear?" McGregor nodded silently, too shocked to do more; he could not really, even now, comprehend the enormous scale of his utter defeat. "Now, get out of my house!"

So saying, Arthur spun him around and delivered a hefty kick to McGregor's backside which was quickly followed by an equally painful blow to the back of his head from the hand of the King. McGregor limped toward the exit, only to have the King's Equerry followed by the footman deliver another kick to his rump, and so on, all the way to the exit gate; every ten metres a footman delivered him with a savage kick up the backside.

Eventually he emerged from the Palace bruised and barely able to walk. In the distance, his eyes beheld the smoking ruin of his seat of power. The Bee Hive was no more! All around him should have been his Defenders, whom he could have rallied to stage a comeback, but every guard was now wearing an Army uniform and a hostile expression and his transport too was gone. The Prime Minister of Great Britain slowly limped his way to the front gate of Buckingham Palace and walked away down The Mall.

Chapter Twenty-Two: Stage Three

Every night for the past week, a man had slipped inside the formidable security fences and quietly poured a drum of liquid into the waters of the Tittesworth West and East Reservoirs, which served the needs of the North London Super Dome. This action was repeated every night for the next seven nights. Likewise, all around the country, every major city's water supply had a visitor for seven nights.

The programme was duplicated in every major world city. There were few discoveries of the intruders, and chemical inspections in the water plants could not detect the additives from the drums; it was the beginning of a silent war, stage three.

There were almost no side effects from the introduced synthetic KP formula; a very few complained of persistent headaches for a while but they dissipated after three days' ingestion of the water based compounds. The most common complaint was that they felt thirstier after drinking the water, and the national water intake increased significantly. One wag in the Angels Network even suggested that KP be introduced into the breweries water also; that way beer sales would be up.

The increase in the intensity of the iris' colour began to be seen after three days of dosing. There was some discussion of the phenomena in public forums and medical online discussion groups, but the general consensus was that it might be some sort of virus, which was evidently harmless otherwise. The unexpected result by the fifth day was a fall in the crime rate; it was postulated by the Angels' doctors that this was due to an increase in awareness by members of the Public; handbag snatchers, for example, were invariably prevented from committing the crime by the actions of passers-by who obstructed a would-be thief from making his dash for the purse. By the seventh day there was widespread awareness and thieves and murderers were actually turning themselves in to the Defenders, confessing their crimes voluntarily. They were tormented by their own memories and could not stop broadcasting their secrets to the people about them; their only remedy was to turn themselves in for justice and absolution or else they would have to face a lynch mob.

The Stewart brothers also observed the changes gradually coming over them. For them there was no fear of the unknown, for the Hokaida sisters, as they called them teasingly, had already absorbed all the benefits of KP and there was a communion between them that defied the laws of close relationship by blood. There seemed to be an intuitive understanding between the ladies that had to be based in some telepathic link, albeit at a lower level than the full telepath abilities of the three children; it was as if they could only unconsciously send and receive, but it was seldom successful if they exerted conscious thought.

The group developed a sort of parlour game between them; one would think of an object or a word and the others would try to get the answer; guessing was not allowed and no clues were given; initially, their failures brought gales of laughter all round, but there was a shocked silence when on the third day of Stage Three, Bill provided the correct answer. They knew then that there was to be no going back. So, from that time onward they all made it a practice to exercise the ability as best they could, and improvement did come to them the more they practiced.

Chapter Twenty-Three: When You Sup With the Devil…

Yuri Galenko was still in London Central, recent events had postponed his trade talks with the Euro Zone, but Yuri was an optimist that they would happen soon and meanwhile he was sure that something would still come up that would 'give him an edge' in the talks. Yuri was a patient man; experience had taught him well on his climb to power.

He had more power in his hands than an ordinary Trade Commissioner might be expected to hold. Every misdemeanour of his bosses, every favour extended to clean up their messes; they all went into Yuri's 'little book' (although the 'little book' actually filled a fair-sized safe, which Yuri kept in a secure location). Yuri believed in serendipity and fortune was about to smile upon him yet again.

The blacked-out limousine cruised along The Mall and came alongside a stumbling man who appeared to be labouring in the heat of the noonday sun.

"Good morning, Mr Prime Minister. Out for your constitutional, are you? But it is very hot now. May I extend you the courtesy of a lift, sir?"

Ian McGregor turned to recognize the face of Yuri Galenko, who smiled at him from the back seat of the limousine. The icy cold blast of the

175

limousine's air conditioner reached the sidewalk where Ian McGregor stood.

"What a kind offer," McGregor called back. "It seems that my transport has been delayed and I could wait no longer!"

"Quite so, quite so," Yuri consoled him, "and I am sure that the events down the road must be very upsetting for you also!" McGregor climbed into the soft luxury of the limousine and accepted the proffered wet towelette and some cologne to refresh himself. The limousine purred along.

"It is indeed fortunate that we met like this; as a matter of fact, I was going to call you and invite you along to my club for a chat," Yuri smoothly lied.

"You have a club here in London?" McGregor asked in surprise.

"Why, of course. We always need places for discreet conversations, in connection with trade matters, you understand." McGregor didn't believe a word of it, but the welcome relief from the unseasonal April heat and the promise of a cool drink swayed him, so they rode together amicably, like old friends, to Yuri's club in West London.

They decided to have lunch too and after gulping down an ice-cold lager, they went through into the members' dining area. The club was almost deserted at this hour; most members would pop in for a drink and a cigar after close of business, but it was only the diehards who frequented the club during the one to three p.m. period.

The menu was basically just English food with some European dishes to loosely qualify as an 'International Cuisine', so choosing was quite simple; they both chose a grilled beef steak with French fries and vegetables. As it turned out, the meat was well cooked, and they got stuck in with relish. Eventually, they laid down their knives and forks with a contented feeling.

"You know," said McGregor, "all these diplomatic lunches and dinners that we are obliged to attend, with all of the chef's fancy creations, seldom leave one with the feeling of having had a proper meal!"

"Quite so," agreed Yuri. Indeed, this was going even better than he had hoped; why, they were practically buddies now!

They retired to a discreet corner of the members' lounge and the waiter served them coffee and chocolate mints. When he had left them, Yuri decided that this might be the right time to play his fish.

"Ian," he opened familiarly, "one couldn't help noticing the awful mess that someone has made of your office building… indeed it is so fortunate that you were out of the building when it happened!" McGregor nodded and waited, not sure what was coming next. "We may be able to help, you know." It was said in such a matter of fact tone that one might have been excused for missing its import but Yuri never wasted his words, and McGregor realized with a jolt that here was someone who wanted to deal. Yes, let's deal!

"Yuri, old chap, your offer is most kind. What kind of help do you have in mind, and what can I do for you in exchange?" McGregor parried him. This was a game, after all, one well understood by both sides.

Yuri decided to surprise McGregor with a direct approach; "Ian, my sources tell me that you are facing a lot of domestic opposition and I have it in my power to make it disappear!"

"How so?" McGregor asked, as he tacitly endorsed Yuri's statement of the status quo; a fact that Yuri did not miss.

"Since the upheavals of the last century and the nuclear disarmament treaties that saw the Russian Federation, Europe and America strip themselves of any real military power, we have all competed in different fields. Euro Zone has grown rich and frankly quite lazy; you have relied upon advanced weaponry and high technology to give you a cushion of security. The Russian Federation, however, has struggled to match you and we are rich in only two areas; resources and people. That is why we are here now. We have been quietly rebuilding our military machine; only conventional weapons of course, because we are honouring our pledges under the Strategic Nuclear Disarmament Treaties. We now have considerable leverage that may be applied against your pathetic British Forces; for example, your forces couldn't even resist an invasion across the British Channel and I dare say that the Joint Chiefs of Staff have resisted your orders to hold strategic war games in the North Sea?"

McGregor sat back in his seat, shocked at the direct affront against his integrity, but also impressed with the accuracy of the Russian's intel; this was no Trade Commissioner!

"Are you suggesting that I sell out my country, sir?" he asked, somewhat self-righteously. "Why, I am a patriot first of all, sir!"

Yuri waved his hands in a deprecating gesture. "No, no, of course not! I am merely suggesting that you do what is best for your country and we will give you the support that you require. We shall simply mass troops along the border to apply pressure upon the British Forces to desist from their attempted coup. In exchange, all we require is your energy, at a much-discounted rate of course! There is no suggestion that we would ever cross the borders of Euro Zone, it's merely chess moves!"

McGregor considered the proposal and its inherent dangers. Finally he said, "We may have a deal, but subject to details of course and the agreement of Herschel and Francois."

Yuri was delighted, and leapt to his feet to shake hands. "Yes!" he said, "we shall all profit by this; it is good for both of our federations and for peace too, of course. Let us put this into action quickly. The World Council Conference is in two days only and we need time to make the troop deployments."

McGregor agreed with a simple "Yes!" and a nod of his head. They sealed their new relationship with a drink, and then each departed on his own way.

Chapter Twenty-Four: A Dance with the Devil

A hasty videoconference was called between the Euro Zone partners. As expected, Herschel was most cautious, but he was also pragmatic. He had been most concerned to see the bombing of the Bee Hive, and to hear of the remarkable turnaround in the King's health and the news that there was an heir to the throne in Prince Arthur. These were all developments that needed a drastic solution; he was mostly concerned about the possibility of a domino effect; there were plenty of contenders just waiting in the wings that would be delighted for the opportunity to bring down the axis and reassert old nationalism. Francois agreed with Herschel, but mostly because he feared public exposure of his profiteering and the use of slave labour for his own interests, and that of his clique of nobles. There were many who had a lot to lose if the axis should fall!

But could the Russians be trusted? What was to stop them from rolling over the borders into Poland and Czechoslovakia? Yes, they needed leverage for insurance against just such a scenario.

Herschel suddenly grinned and reached for the comm. link, "Hold it for a moment, guys!" he said.

A few moments later he was back. "There is an old suitcase nuclear dirty bomb network, a leftover from the 2070's. The core cell was planted in Moscow by our operatives. We only need to send one signal and it will act as a comm. link to activate a series of similar bombs all over the Russian Federation. It is a doomsday weapon of course, but America and Russia survived for decades on the MAD policy, that is Mutually Assured Destruction. It worked for them, and it will work for us the same way. Naturally, the weapons net can only be effective when the other party knows about its existence. We will make sure that Mr. Yuri Galenko does get to hear this piece of intelligence!"

Francois asked, "Are we sure that it will work now, after all these years?"

"Not a chance in Hell, actually!" Herschel responded quite cheerfully, "the batteries were probably finished long ago, but we don't need to tell them that; it's a huge bluff really, but can he afford to call us on it?" They all laughed heartily, mostly out of relief; good old Herschel, what a brain!

Ian wasted no time in giving the news to Yuri, who was first ecstatic and then furious when he heard about the bomb network that was sitting in Russia. "Ian, how could you betray our friendship in this way? I gave you my personal assurance that we would never cross Euro Zone's borders!"

"I know, Yuri," McGregor replied easily, "but as you said earlier; 'it's just chess moves'. That's all it is: chess and business, that's all!"

Yuri sighed. "Alright, let me speak with Moscow; it seems we have raised MAD from the dead! Didn't history teach us anything?" he asked.

"Yes, indeed," McGregor replied, "it was CYA; 'cover your arse!'" With that Ian McGregor closed the connection.   He carried with him a lasting image of Yuri's stony expression.   He mused; to sup with the Devil, you need to bring a long spoon, but to dance with the Devil, wear steel toecaps.

Chapter Twenty-Five: A New Strategy

At GHQ strategic command, the satellite images were coming in showing Russian mass troop movements towards the Euro Zone eastern borders. The movement was on a massive scale, unlike anything seen for over thirty years.

Field Marshal Miller was notified and he immediately called an emergency meeting of the Joint Chiefs of Staff; then, he placed all UK air, sea and ground forces on a state of high alert. It was only a precaution of course, but Euro Central was only a day's drive by a Russian mechanized division, once it had crossed the Polish border.

From the command centre, he spoke with his counterparts in France and Germany. As expected, their state of readiness was even worse than that of the British Forces, having being denied funding for even replacement of men, maintenance of equipment and acquisition of assets that would be required in a war scenario.

"Those damn politicians!" he swore.

The council of war discussed the options available; there were actually very few. General Spencer wondered about the timing of this.

"Why now? There had been no provocations from Euro Zone, in fact weren't there supposed to be some trade talks going on, right now, here in London Central?"

Air Chief Commodore Graves agreed and added, "Gentlemen, I smell a rat; a very small Scottish rat, to be sure!"

This deduction changed everything.

"Now what, another object lesson?" asked General Harvey.

"Yes, indeed!" Field Marshall Miller replied, "But this time I think it is our wily Russians that need the lesson!" Lt. Col Ballantyne was called over. "John, can you arrange for something to detonate in or very near the Russian Embassy in London Central? I think tomorrow would be most appropriate. And make sure that it has the Defenders' ID all over it! This should ensure that this alliance is short-lived!"

"Consider it done, sir!" Ballantyne replied with a big grin.

At eight o'clock in the morning, on the last day before the World Council Conference was due to begin, a large parcel bomb with a shaped charge was detonated at the gates of the Russian Embassy. The force of the explosion blew the gates right off and hurled them through the ground floor windows of the Embassy; every other window was also shattered by the blast. There was no damage to adjacent properties because the direction of the shaped charge had directed the explosion directly toward the Embassy's front door. The Bomb squad investigators would find an hour later several small clues that pointed inexorably to the Defenders Brigade.

Monitoring equipment had been activated by the Army; the subject of the eavesdropping was Ian McGregor. An unencrypted call was recorded by the monitors only five minutes after the blast. Voice identification software identified the caller as Yuri Galenko; he was very, very upset.

"You bastard! Is this what you call a partnership? I know it was you who planted that bomb! I'm covered in cuts from that flying glass and my suit is all cut to pieces! No, don't try to deny it; I'm sure that it was you. You are crazy to do this. Do you think that I'm going to lay down and let you roll over me, *over me*? I'll tell you what I think; I think I'm going to make a few calls. One of them will be to your GHQ, and I will speak with Field Marshal Miller himself. Yes, that is what I'm gonna do! By the time that he's finished with you, you will be lucky to avoid a firing squad; I've got you on tape you know? He'll charge you with treason, you fool! I will make the same deal with your opposition; they will have sense enough not to bait the bear! You're finished, McGregor, finished!"

The recording of the conversation and the transcript were sent up to the Command Centre and passed immediately to the Field Marshall, who read the transcript slowly and with some satisfaction.

"And game, set and match, my friend!" He called up John Ballantyne. "John, I have some interesting new documentation and recordings that you ought to see. We shall need to keep these for the trial of Ian McGregor. I'll leave it to you to do the follow up with Yuri Galenko; after May the first would be best, I think. "

Chapter Twenty-Six: Final Preparations

At the Stewart Farm everyone had been anticipating the arrival of Jack Bailey for his final briefing. Just what they had in mind for the children to do still had to be spelled out. Jim naturally didn't want them to be put into any personal danger, but it was clear that destiny had an appointment with them at the World Council Conference, which was scheduled for the First of May, at the London International Conference Centre.

Jack Bailey arrived on time, at five p.m., this time with a convoy of Army Staff ground cars flying the pennants of the High Command. This raised much excitement with the children and more than a little curiosity with the adults; they had expected the usual low key, cloak and dagger kind of meeting that they'd had last time, but not this... and what was the Army doing here? Had something gone very wrong?

Jack Bailey stepped out of the leading staff car, which was a limousine. To everyone's complete surprise, he was in a military uniform and he bore the rank insignia of a Lt. Colonel!

"Allow me to introduce myself," he said to the shell-shocked group before him. "My name is John Ballantyne, Lt. Colonel John Ballantyne. I am attached to the staff of Field Marshal David Miller at GHQ, Sandhurst." Then, stepping aside, he said, "May I introduce Field Marshall Miller? I know that he has been dying to make your acquaintance."

The other rear side door of the limousine opened and Field Marshall Miller stepped out and offered his hand. "Hello," he said, "I am David Miller, and I'm thrilled to meet with you all!"

Jim replied, "Likewise, I'm sure. Well, let's go inside"

The small party entered the central cottage and they all made themselves comfortable. Jim started the introductions; "May I present our first arrivals, Sakura and Grace, and this is Akemi, Ren, Akiyoshi and Asuka. And these are my brothers Bill and John. Quite a houseful, as you can see; and with three four year olds running around, getting into all sorts of mischief, quite a handful too!"

Sakura made some tea and everyone sat around again to hear what John Ballantyne had to say. He began by apologizing.

"First of all, I'm sorry for the misdirection earlier; the Angel Network is a civilian resistance movement and they have formed links worldwide. It was thought that although we share the same goals, some members of the Network would not trust the military, so my subterfuge was necessary. We have been quietly orchestrating the resistance here and providing unmarked equipment and some logistical support, but mostly they have achieved a lot on their own and it has been through their independent efforts; we as a nation owe them a great debt. For a similar reason, the sympathies of the Armed Forces for the Angel Network's cause had to be concealed from the spies of the Defenders; only now are we openly defying the Prime Minister, and, as you have probably heard, we destroyed the Bee Hive yesterday by an aerial bombardment; which means that the eyes and ears of the Euro Zone triumvirate are closed, and they are fatally crippled now. I should also like to add that the brain behind all of this has been Field Marshal Miller, he came up with the strategy and I, being relatively an unknown, was able to pass myself off as 'Jack Bailey', and I rose to lead the Angel Network. One other further piece of information that I can pass on is that His Majesty, King Charles the Fourth, is one hundred per cent behind all of this, and also that there is an Heir Apparent; Prince Arthur, whom we have protected until now. His Majesty was subjected to years of poisoning that deprived him of full mobility and communication; McGregor wanted him to be unable to rally the people against his regime, and we have no doubt whatsoever that it was McGregor's intention to eventually assassinate the King and declare a Republic. Happily, that plan was prevented and we were able to stop the drugging of His Majesty and to treat the King with KP; fortunately he is fully recovered, perhaps even better than before the drugging started! You might also be pleased to hear that my Palace sources have informed us that Ian McGregor was quite literally booted out of Buckingham Palace yesterday, after being forced to watch the demolition of his beloved Bee Hive building!

David Miller took up the narration. "He immediately attempted to strike a deal with the Russians, effectively committing treason. We shall present fully incriminating evidence when he is brought to trial. No doubt there will be many prominent politicians and businessmen who will have to account for their misdeeds and collaboration during the regimes of Ian McGregor, Francois Bernard and Herschel Schwartz! The process will take some time, but we are most keen that justice will be seen to be done. Now, as to current events; these three amazing children have been brought across the world at great risk to themselves and to others who helped them; I don't know how many have died to protect this secret, but we owe a debt to them to see this through. The key event is tomorrow; at the World Council Conference, which is scheduled for First of May, at the London International Conference Centre. It is a sign of how important this event is, in that, in spite of the civil unrest and military rebellion, here in England, the very site of the venue, not a single world leader has cancelled his attendance. We believe that our action tomorrow will prevent them reaching an accord that will enslave the whole of mankind for the foreseeable future!"

Everyone gasped at the last statement. It was Jim Stewart who eventually spoke up, shattering the silence that lay heavy in the room.

"You have solid evidence of what you say?" Miller nodded silently, his eyes locked on to Stewart's. "OK, then," said Jim, "what do you want the children to do? I can't say yes or no; it will have to be a joint decision with their mothers."

"Agreed and understood completely, Jim," John Ballantyne interjected, "Field Marshal Miller has always stressed that he would only take it to stage four if, and only if, everyone was of a single mind on this. Please forgive the pun," he added with a smile. He continued, "Simply put, we want the children to change the leaders' minds, send them home with a new perspective that will benefit the whole of mankind as it grows into the kind of telepathic society that we are dreaming of."

"And what if they resist? What will be the consequences?" asked Sakura.

David Miller took the question. "That, my dear, is the big question! We just don't know enough about the kind of stress that a human mind can endure. We do know that it broke the sanity of the E.A.R.'s chief assassin, Chen Li; he's the one that the children confronted at the Priddy Circles. We hope that it won't come to that, but consider this, what are the minds of a few monsters and despots compared to the billions that they will enslave for generations?"

Again there was another silence. It was Ren who spoke. "We will go into the bedroom to discuss your words now, and when we return you shall have your answer."

While Jim and the three mothers discussed the issues, Bill offered to show John Ballantyne and David Miller the underground laboratory. They all went down the steps.

Bill related how they lured first the Defenders and then the Chinese squads into the trap. Bill explained that the gas only took seconds to kill the intruders; it had been included in their designs only as an afterthought, but now they were very glad that they went for that option; it had certainly saved the lives of everybody on the Farm. Young John demonstrated the escape capsules and the control systems and David Miller and John Ballantyne were most impressed.

"How come we allowed you guys to leave the forces? You would have been such an asset to us!" David Miller asked.

The tour completed, they all trooped back into the living room, the sisters and Jim were waiting for them.

Jim spoke up. "You are sure that the children will be under your protection at all times?" David Miller gave his word. "In that case, it's all clear! May we accompany the children to the Conference?"

"Definitely!" David Miller replied, "in any case, your expertise with descanning the security systems will be invaluable. We shall take care of the manual guards. By the way, how does this descanner of yours work? We tried for a long time but we couldn't manage to neutralize the scanning systems."

Dr. Jim Stewart replied, "Well actually, the technology is a modification of a principle that has been known about for a long time; 'EMP', or electro-magnetic pulses, which occur whenever you have a large release of energy, such as a

191

rapidly changing magnetic flux, as in a nuclear explosion. As you probably are aware, EMP knocks out every live electrical device in its range. That wouldn't be very useful as a descanner; for one thing, it requires a huge amount of power, a large converter and a conveyance the size of a transporter pod just to carry it. Security might smell a rat if they saw one of those parked nearby! Electromagnetic weapons, or E-bombs, release a high-power flash of radio waves or microwaves. Depending on the energy of the EMP, this may disable electronic circuitry or create physiological effects in those exposed to the pulse."

"The pulse released by an electromagnetic weapon lasts for an extremely short time, around one ten-billionth of a second. The physiological effects of the EMP microwave radiation on humans have been studied too; if directed at someone at a range of two hundred metres, the body temperature can be raised up to forty two degrees from thirty seven degrees. In the late twentieth century, some military researchers actually produced microwave weapons. There is a device called the Pulse Wave Myotron which is commercially available in Britain. It emits rapid pulses of electromagnetic radiation that paralyse the voluntary muscles of someone caught in the beam by disturbing the electrical pulses that normally flow between the nerves within the voluntary muscles. For example, a person caught in the beam is unable to move or speak for up to 30 minutes, which is the time it takes the muscles to regain their normal polarity.

"So, you see, my device had to be non-lethal, portable and effective for a practical range. We settled on five hundred metres maximum line of sight range, but the shorter the range, the less power is consumed, so we recommend short bursts of EMP at perhaps fifty metres range where scanners are visible, and one to two hundred where remote scanners are suspected."

"Now as the manufacturer of Stewart Scanners, I have detailed knowledge of the frequencies at which each device operates, so my descanner can select only those particular frequencies to jam. The power problem I solved by first of all restricting the range of the descanner and then using the miniature fuel packs that are used in robots. The life of the fuel pack is limited of course, but we do recharge them from solar cell chargers before every mission; they are definitely a short term solution until you can provide me miniature nuclear fuel packs!"

Jim decided to ask John Ballantyne a follow up question for everyone's interest; "You say that the Defenders' communications are pretty well degraded; are they going to be solely responsible for security at the Conference Centre? What about private contractors employed by some of the delegations, won't they also have their own levels of screening?"

"Good question, Jim. Yes, some of the bigger delegations will have their own security or employ private contractors," John Ballantyne replied. "We shall use that to infiltrate in some areas, but these days most governments rely heavily upon electronic surveillance; we can degrade their surveillance systems also, in fact we have already, but they just don't know it yet! Jim, we have been preparing for years for this opportunity, things may go a little wrong but we do have back up plans in place too!"

"Yes, you could always bomb the place if all else fails!" John Stewart quipped. The look on the faces of David Miller and John Ballantyne surprised him. "Oh, Oh! You would, wouldn't you?"

"Yes, John; in the last extreme, we would!"

It was agreed that the whole party would travel up to London Central that evening; John Ballantyne would arrange aerial transportation and in the morning they would infiltrate the Conference Centre. The World Council Conference proper would begin only in the afternoon. The morning session would be for a pomp and glory speech by the outgoing Chairman, followed by an introductory Press Conference and then lunch for the delegates and their staff. The Centre had a capacity of twenty thousand people, but fifteen thousand only were expected to attend the opening programme.

Chapter Twenty-Seven: The Great Leader

Long Wei was a scion of an important trading family that gained its wealth during the days after the fall of the Communist Party in China. In those days, many entrepreneurs became dollar billionaires by opportunistic exploitation of a huge domestic market and manufacturing of foreign goods under license. Through the latter, the Wei Corporation gained much technology without having to do the tedious research and development that their foreign partners had to do.

Wei Corp, as it was known, mainly manufactured all manner of electronics for both the retail and military markets. Inevitably they moved into their own R&D, and Long Wei's special interest was the marriage between electronics and robotics.

From 2070 onwards, artificial intelligence had advanced from a plaything of academics to a commercial property that Wei Corp could exploit for a great profit. Wei Corp began producing robots for every industrial need. Its systems controls were developed in-house and rivalled anything that could be produced in the Euro Zone. Long Wei was mad about cybernetics and robotics; some said that it was the clinical logic of the programming that appealed most of all to him.

With the development of the first positronic brain in 2085, the role of the robot advanced from merely a mechanical slave with limited programmed functions to that of a reasoning servant. For some this gave cause for alarm, but Long Wei embraced it; he felt that ultimately the destiny of the human race had to be merged with the robotic so that it could shake off its physical weaknesses.

Life looked good for Long Wei; by his thirtieth birthday, he was immensely rich, able to choose whatever he wanted to do, and he was courted by the rich and famous to endorse their projects or a candidacy. Women didn't interest him too much; they were too emotional to suit his tastes. Occasionally, he would indulge himself with a woman hired for a night, but that was out of necessity; a weakness in himself that he secretly loathed.

China's decision to annex the former tiger economies of the Asian region was opportunistic; in business you had to know the right moment. When your rival was weakened; that was the time to strike. The East Asian Republic, or E.A.R., was born, but the old party leadership lacked the vitality of youth to consolidate and exploit the windfall of the economic collapse of Asia following the Great Seismic Disaster of the 2050's.

He decided to enter politics, while his younger brother Hu Wei took over the running of the Wei Empire. Within five years, Long Wei had eclipsed the old guard of the People's Party and he was seen as the natural heir to the leadership. China had never embraced the multi-party system of the Western democracies, and capitalism existed within a one party state; it suited China and the E.A.R. Then tragedy struck Long Wei, such as what could have befallen any ordinary man.

He was walking past a construction site in Beijing; they were using robotic machines for demolition of the old structures on the site. One of the machines malfunctioned and collided with another; then, spinning out of control, the robot ploughed across the walkway, running over Long Wei as it careened into the street.

Long Wei was critically injured; his right arm and leg were left hanging by a thread and the left side of his skull was crushed. Doctors who examined him at the Beijing Trauma Centre determined that he had damage to his left frontal lobe as well as the left side of his brain. The damage to his right arm and leg necessitated surgical removal, and the brain damage was expected to impair his sequential functions, such as language and mathematics, while the frontal lobe damage was expected to result in the loss of the ability to control his emotional behaviour.

To a less determined man this accident would have consigned them to a living hell, but Long Wei prevailed upon his brother Hu to allow him enter into a course of surgery that was so ground-breaking that few would have entertained it; he would become a cyborg!

Advances in surgical techniques had made it possible to replace the damaged left side of his brain with a positronic one, which was then grafted into his remaining natural brain. His damaged limbs were replaced with prostheses, or bionically

197

powered limbs. The positronic graft was not perfect; he had to make do with an imperfect bionic ear, for example, which gave irregular amplification of sounds; but he was alive and functioning.

The convalescence period was two years, and then another two years of rehabilitation; learning to master new skills. Eventually, the day came for his return to the world of men; in truth, he felt less like a man than a machine, and while the scars left him with a somewhat fearsome appearance, that caused people to steer away from him, he felt nothing emotionally. Perhaps his changed circumstances, for the first time in his life, had made him feel truly happy.

Contrary to all expectations, he re-entered politics, and he was re-elected to his previous position in the Party. From that time on, Long Wei showed that he was a new man and considered himself not handicapped but enhanced; he was not burdened by sentimental motivations, but the positronic brain was not able to completely subjugate his mood swings.

Long Wei studied the proposed implant that lay in the centre of his palm. It was a small capsule, not five millimetres long and the width of a grain of rice. Early development of the device had been done by IBM and others in the twentieth century. Unfortunately, there was some resistance to its introduction and the technology had remained dormant for a century. Long Wei alone had seen the potential of the technology when it would be merged with twenty first century developments in robotics and systems of control.

Within this small device existed a circuitry chip that had the means to solve several chronic societal problems. The capsule contained a RFID passive device that would respond to a scanner with full details of the bearer, his financial dealings, his health records, even his current location. It could be fitted with a solar-rechargeable lithium ion battery, so that the device could be configured to administer certain psychotropic drugs or pain stimuli from a remote controller. No one would be able to conduct any transactions without being scanned. Financial frauds would be prevented because this control system would usher in a cashless society.

The implant was to be inserted under the skin by means of a simple modified syringe instrument. His researchers had concluded that since the device would have to recharge its lithium-ion battery from solar radiation for some of its functions, and for ease of access, the optimum placement would be in the back of the subject's right hand or alternatively on the forehead.

Initially, it would be proposed to the World Council as a universal device to prevent credit card fraud and identity theft, but the implications and full potential of the technology would not be immediately apparent to governments. This was the perfect instrument of control, and ultimately the whole world would fall under Long Wei's sovereignty because he would encourage all leaders to personally participate in the use of the implant under the pretext of security. So the whole of mankind would be enslaved and conformed to Long Wei's will!

He didn't doubt that the World Council would endorse his device, because it enabled them to exert a great measure of control over their populations. The chip implant was but the first stage in his grand plan; his ultimate aim was to render every human being into a sort of drone, merged with artificial intelligence and incapable of all but the basest of actions. Like worker ants, they would toil without complaint in exchange for the minimum requirements of life. In short, Long Wei saw this as the only path to lasting world peace.

Long Wei was in London Central, at the E.A.R. Embassy. The Conference would begin tomorrow; it was to be his glorious moment in history! But first there was some housekeeping to attend to… he sent for General Chi.

No one who was summoned to the presence of the Great Leader could fail to be intimidated by him. Physically, he was a freak. His prosthetic bionic left eye stared back at you with a passionless intensity. Long Wei was invariably connected to a computer network via a cable to an implanted terminal in his positronic brain; while he conversed, his right hand flashed at blinding speed across a mini keypad as he processed multiple queries simultaneously while he conversed. There was no doubt that the Great Leader was a freak, but he was also an extremely well informed one.

Long Wei sat behind the desk in a high backed chair with armrests. At his right side a keypad rested, and as usual his right hand was flashing across the keys. "General Chi!" He spoke in his soft voice, "thank you for coming to see me. I wanted to go over the security reports. Please sit in the chair opposite me." He indicated a chair identical to his own.

General Chi felt a little encouraged in being asked to sit; this might not be as bad as he'd expected. "Indeed sir," General Chi nervously replied, "is there anything wrong or incomplete in my screening arrangements for the Conference?"

"Well, no. It's not about that. I am going over the Chen Li reports. Have you seen them all?" Long Wei asked, in his deceptively gentle manner.

"Yes, sir, I believe that I have." The General now was becoming decidedly uncomfortable; would he never be rid of this incompetent Chen Li?

"Well, I have been reading the whole history of this sad Hokaida affair, from the file's beginning in Incheon, Korea. The story began with him fighting us as an International Force volunteer; then, we allowed him to escape to Kyoto, Japan, where he resumed his research into genetics, with that American wife, Dr Glenda Woods. Am I correct so far?"

Chi nodded. A lump formed in his throat.

Long Wei continued, "Now, according to the records forwarded to me by Chen Li, he advised you against a frontal assault of the Hokaida residence. As a result of disregarding his advice,

201

by the time that you gained entry to the laboratory, Hokaida was dead, stabbed by yourself in the back it is reported, and his wife and daughter had escaped. They left behind only some diaries and some unidentified fluid in the safe. I may add that your team destroyed whatever evidence might have been in the safe by recklessly blowing the door. Furthermore, the reports indicated that Hokaida's nieces were involved in some experiments that he and his wife were conducting, and they also escaped. Chen Li suggests that they were working on viral agents to be used against us."

"Now we come to your manhunt. Your men tracked one of the nieces to an airfield in Turkey; a joint military and civilian base at Kocaali. This E.A.R. team killed a Russian team who were also hunting the niece, thereby drawing unwanted attention from Euro Zone Security Deputy Director, Wolf Braun. Then Chen Li made a breakthrough and traced all of the missing Hokaida clan women to a farm in Somerset, England. At this farm your crack assassins were somehow defeated by a team of three farmers, three women and three four-year-old children! Chen Li himself escaped the fate of his team and reached this Embassy in a distressed condition, where your doctor diagnosed Chen Li as being insane; and he has been committed to an institution for the mentally insane in Beijing. I may have glossed over some points in this sad tale of incompetence, but do you agree that the facts are substantively correct?"

General Chi weakly nodded his head.

"Gentlemen, please come forward." Long Wei spoke to the medical technician and three security personnel who had silently entered the room. "General Chi," he resumed in his soft tone, "you are about to render me a great service!"

"Of course, sir!" Chi exclaimed, "Whatever I can do to help you."

At this, the security guards moved quickly forward and applied restraints that pinned General Chi's arms and legs to the chair. A leather strap was placed about his head and affixed to the high backed chair. Chi, terrified about what was to come, sat struggling against the restraints but they were securely fixed and resistance was useless.

"General Chi, I am engaged upon some research. Our nation is about to make a giant leap forward. I have it in my power to chemically suppress the unwanted emotions and undirected thinking that has characterized the Chinese people and prevented us from achieving our destiny. You are going to be the first to follow the path that I blazed. With this injection into your left frontal lobe you will be a candidate for a positronic implant; don't fear it! You will be freed from all negative emotions and the incoherence of thought that led you to make so many important mistakes."

He nodded to the doctor who raised his syringe and advanced toward the General. General Chi saw what he carried in his hand and he screamed, and he kept on screaming. Long Wei looked on dispassionately with evident interest. Eventually,

Chi's eyes rolled upward and he lapsed into a catatonic state.

"Prepare him for transportation to Beijing!" Long Wei ordered. He resumed his tapping of the keys on the keypad.

Chapter Twenty-Eight: The World Council Conference

The London Central Conference Centre, or LCCC as it was known commonly, was a world-class venue where major political forums and annual conferences were hosted. The World Council met annually, and this year it was the turn of Britain to be the host nation.

Since the demise of the United Nations in the upheaval years of the 2060's, the World Council was the principal platform for international questions to be discussed. It was customary for the leading blocs to be given preference in tabling their issues and this year the E.A.R. had raised the issues of security and financial control. The leader of the E.A.R., Long Wei, in one of his rare public appearances, would be personally putting forward what he described as the final solution that would solve both questions at a stroke. The presentation was eagerly awaited by all leaders.

The LCCC was a showcase for the best in British architecture, so Ian McGregor was pinning his hopes on regaining some prestige that the recent turmoil throughout the Euro Zone had lost the partnership. He was pulling out all the stops to present Britain at its best. The building was large, having a seated capacity of twenty thousand. It was in the form of a huge syntho-glass bubble set over a square base. The base comprised six floors of offices, conference centres for medium to small groups, translation centres and Press and media communications hubs. Three floors of the base were below ground level. Above the base was the main auditorium, which was arranged in tiered concentric circles with an atrium of blue syntho glass. Huge projection screens were arranged so that every participant could view the chief speaker, and simultaneous voice-over translation was seamlessly transmitted in fifty languages to the delegates.

Security was made extremely tight, as might be expected where so many world leaders were gathered together under one roof. The delegates and technical staff were constrained to pass through several checkpoints, where they were scanned and sniffed by electronic sniffers and trained sniffer dogs. They were also subjected to voice and facial recognition examination, retina and fingerprint analysis; it was the best that could be done to ensure that only the approved persons would be able to enter the auditorium and technical suites within the base area. After examination, every person would be issued a RFID tag, which was to be worn on the outer garment. The tags were reissued every day so that duplication was impossible; also re-admittance was not possible the same day.

This was the environment that the Angels Network were about to penetrate; with three children included in the party, it seemed impossible that they would gain access at the front doors, let alone get past the tiered security checks.

Major John Ballantyne, Jim Stewart and the Hokaida family stood together on the plaza before the LCCC. Already, members of the Press, invited members of the public and delegates were queuing at the first security barrier for their security passes, so that they could avoid the longer wait of the latecomers.

Dr Jim raised this burning question with John Ballantyne. "Major, seeing that there is going to be extra vigilance because of the Angels' attacks, won't we encounter every conceivable kind of screening; thermal, biometric, X-ray, ultrasound and not forgetting cameras equipped with facial recognition ability and manual inspections by expert personnel; just how do you propose to overcome all these levels of security? I can deal with the scanners, but when all of these systems are operating simultaneously..."

"Yes, Jim," John replied, "as I said before, we have been preparing for this event with the same thoroughness that we would do for a military war game." John continued, "You have rightly put your finger on a crucial element; beating the multiple systems. The answer is deceptively simple: layering! We divide the attack into layers. Layer number one — electronic scanning systems; these you will take out using your EMP descanner. Layer number two — cameras equipped with facial recognition software links to a central computer system; these we will take out; we infiltrated the LCCC control centre and camera surveillance over six months ago. We are able to control what they see, and by feeding pre-recorded loops of earlier activity into the LCCC monitors. What they see will be normal movements that will raise no flags. We are also able to control what is seen and heard within the auditorium. And, finally, layer number three — expert search and security personnel who man every checkpoint and gate that we pass through, and patrol the corridors looking for people like us. These the children will handle. Have you instructed them what their role is for today?" he concluded, turning to the ladies.

"Major," Sakura affirmed, "these may look like normal four-year-olds, but remember they carry an awareness which has been genetically enhanced and the memories and experience of Jim and I. They are also incredibly smart. Oh, yes, they certainly understand what is required!"

John smiled and said, "Very well then; let's proceed, troops!"

They dutifully joined the queue, which was moving quite quickly. A few bystanders looked at the children curiously, but assumed that they must be the family of a VIP and said nothing. The first two security guards likewise allowed them to pass unchallenged; they had a sort of faraway look in their eyes that obviously indicated that their minds were in neutral gear for a few moments. Jim activated his descanners; he carried several attached to his belt, each tuned to different wavelength bands used by the various systems.

When they reached the physical search and X-ray gates, the children worked on the staff while Jim took out the surveillance systems. With a smile, the guards presented each of them with the precious ID tags. Following John's lead, they then proceeded to a small auditorium, which was deserted.

"We have cleared all of the main security checks at the base level, but we have yet to penetrate the auditorium," John informed them. "We can expect LCCC and private contractor security to do random checks on ID tags and rooms at this level and upstairs, especially in the auditorium also. Since we have to observe radio silence, we have few means to receive a warning from our technicians who are monitoring the camera security. If a patrol comes this way, we shall hear only two soft buzzes on my comm. link and then it will be up to the children to deal with the intrusion. Is that clear everyone? OK, we have two hours before we need to move again. Let's remain quiet and try to relax; everything is going according to plan. In one hour, they will begin the introductory speeches and welcome and then the conference will adjourn for lunch; that is when we will move. We will hear a cue of three soft buzzes from our monitoring team when it is safe for us to move out."

They settled down in the auditorium seating. The doors were locked as a precaution, but no one expected LCCC security to come along just yet. After half an hour, John's comm. link buzzed softly twice and someone tried the door. Akiyoshi sent the security man an urgent call to go to the main foyer and he left quickly.

Ten minutes later the alarm came again. They could hear a dog sniffing under the door. This time the dog was instructed to lift his leg and they could hear the guard's shout as the urine soaked his trousers. There was the sound of a slap and the dog yelped, and then there was silence at the door.

After two and a quarter hours, the triple buzz signal sounded and they stepped out of their sanctuary and made their way to the elevators in total silence. They reached the elevators and again Jim activated his descanners, while the children broadcasted to the vicinity. Instead of going directly to the auditorium, the lift stopped at the third floor; John's alarm buzzed twice again so they knew something unexpected had happened. The children readied themselves for the intruder.

When the doors opened a tall, grey haired gentleman stepped into the lift; it was Wolf Braun! He showed no sign of recognition at all; in fact he had that same faraway look in his eyes that the guards downstairs had had.

They rode the remaining floor to the auditorium in silence. Wolf Braun seemed to be unaware of the presence of the group in the elevator cabin. Upon reaching the auditorium, he stepped out smartly and went down to the speaker's dais where preparations for the resumption of the conference were already underway.

As planned, they ascended by the steps to the second tier of seating and divided the children so that they were equi-angularly disposed about the circular chamber. Below them, in the centre of the circle, the main delegates and the speaker began to take their places. Above their heads, three gigantic screens broadcast live images of the auditorium.

Presently the screens showed the empty dais of the speaker. The first person to ascend the dais was the Session Chairman, who was the President of the Cameroon Republic. He began to speak, welcoming the delegates back to the first working session of the conference. He reminded the delegates that the first speaker was the Chairman of the East Asian Republic, who would speak in Mandarin, and there would be live translation of his speech into any language that they required, they merely had to wear the headset and select a language from the console in front of them. Each delegate also had his personal monitor in the console but most preferred to watch the session on the large overhead screens.

Long Wei slowly made his way to the dais. Owing to his prosthetic right leg, he didn't walk evenly; he seemed to have a rolling action reminiscent of a sailor home from the sea. He received a warm welcome and a standing ovation from the delegates, which was in reality in deference to his empire's power over many of the countries assembled for the conference. The delegates were seated according to the bloc that they were members of and it was clear that the largest blocs were the E.A.R and the Euro Zone. Indeed the senior members of both blocs had priority seating in the central area of the auditorium. Behind the leaders sat the minor delegates of their bloc.

Long Wei regarded the conference silently for a moment. His cold prosthetic eye gave him an otherworldly look and his right hand twitched nervously, as if looking for its keypad. Having fixed everyone with his baleful look, he cleared his throat in preparation to begin his prepared speech.

As he began to speak, the overhead screens carried footage of scenes of disorder, drug usage, money launderers and various criminal operations. The film also showed the brutal suppression of the disorder by the authorities; Euro Zone as well as E.A.R.

"Mr Chairman, Ladies and Gentlemen, distinguished World Council Conference delegates, it is my honour to come before you at such an hour as this." Long Wei amplified his remarks by pointing to the overhead screens which were now showing, much to the obvious discomfort of Ian McGregor, scenes that showed the bombardment of the Bee Hive building; first the fiftieth floor, followed by its total destruction. "The footage you see was sent to me personally by the very rebels who committed this insurrection; do they have no shame? It is scandalous that a peace-loving government like that of the Euro Zone should have to suffer such attacks upon their sovereignty." Then there followed more footage showing the destruction of Francois Bernard's home and Herschel Schwartz' home-office, both of whom squirmed in their seats in embarrassment. "These attacks were both filmed by nationalistic rebels and they also had the audacity to send me the filmed record of their outrages!"

Long Wei's voice raised its pitch. "Delegates, what you see before you is what happens when our paternalistic benevolence is mistaken for weakness! Governments need to be strong, they also need to be vigilant, but they most of all need the tools to control these unruly elements of society!"

His voice softened. "My friends, the very fabric of our societies is under attack. Money laundering is rampant worldwide; drug smuggling creates tremendous wealth that funds terrorism such you have seen here today; moreover, taxation is avoided, which impoverishes governments and does not allow them to provide for the best welfare of their citizens."

"However, all is not hopeless. My brother's corporation has redeveloped a technology that was lost through the years of turmoil. This technology will return the power and control of our nations to the legitimate governments." These remarks were heartily endorsed by the delegates, who interrupted Long Wei's speech with a five minute standing ovation.

Long Wei now signalled the media team to play the next segment of his presentation. "What you see before you is a device which may be inserted under the skin of the hand or the forehead. It is a simple procedure to insert it and it has been in use for generations already, in a more simplified form of course, to identify animals for export and ownership purposes. It has therefore been shown to be one hundred per cent reliable and foolproof. This more advanced device, which was developed by the Wei Corporation, will carry all details about the bearer. It will replace all credit cards, passports and visa requirements; cash will become obsolete and all transactions will be automatic through RFID technology, and the records will be centralized. It is more efficient and less prone to tampering than any other prime document; the device contains an unique eighteen digit number which will immediately tell the authorities about the place of birth and nationality of the bearer; and finally, as a bonus, the device will provide real-time geo-positional information about the bearer, which will vastly assist the authorities who are hunting down the criminal elements!" He then proceeded to recite the technical specifications for the device and to illustrate how its universal introduction would assist all government agencies in their fight against organized crime and taxation avoidance.

Meanwhile, the Hokaida children were studying Long Wei in puzzlement. Finally, Grace turned to Sakura and whispered, "Mummy, what I sense about this man is so strange. It's as if he is a machine! Half of his brain is human, but the other half is like a robot's brain. We cannot read the machine brain, it is too different, but I sense that it is cold and evil, very evil!"

Sakura replied, "My children, you have correctly read the situation! This man has a grafted robotic brain because his natural brain was damaged in an accident; he also has prosthetic limbs on his right side. By his history, he has shown himself to be possibly the most evil man that has ever lived. He is the reason that you are here. He has to be stopped at all costs! He already rules over half of mankind and has done terrible atrocities to the people of the E.A.R.; no doubt this device is merely a ploy to establish control over the whole of humanity!" Grace sent the whole of this conversation to Akemi and Akiyoshi.

"So, Mummy, what are we to do?" Grace pleaded.

"For now, we wait; John Ballantyne and David Miller will show when you have to act, and if it comes to close quarters combat, your mothers and I are skilled in hand to hand combat techniques!" As if to emphasize the point she showed her the Kyoshi hardened plastic combat knife that she had concealed on her ankle! "We are all carrying weapons, just in case anyone gets too close!"

Long Wei reached the climax of his speech, his voice, normally soft, now raged. He cursed the rebellious people who had forced him to suppress the societies of the E.A.R. They were to blame for the starvation that threatened the populations of the world; because of their provocations, government funds had to be diverted to investment in armaments and security forces... he went on and on, a diatribe that revealed that he was quite unhinged.

He was so caught up in his emotional finale that he didn't notice that above his head the screens were now showing a picture of himself, a caricature in the form of a donkey. The donkey brayed and shook its head from side to side, mouthing the words, 'Liar, liar!'

Then there followed a refutation of the claims that Long Wei had been making at such length. The text kept rolling. It explained that the devices had the power to control the wearer through subcutaneous release of strong drugs which would render him unable to function as a thinking individual; that all control over money would revert to Long Wei because he had the master key to the system; that every person on the face of the Earth would be enslaved forever; lifeless drone workers forced to do whatever their master Long Wei demanded!

The donkey brayed again and again, but this time the words, "Liar, liar!" were transmitted over the audio speakers; over and over, the whole world heard the words that condemned Long Wei as the monster that he was.

Seeing the delegates openly laughing at him, Long Wei became enraged and he stopped speaking in shocked disbelief. Such a thing had never, could *never* happen to him! Then, hearing the words "Liar, liar!" being blared out, his face contorted into the most evil expression of rage and he beat repeatedly on the lectern with his prosthetic right hand until the wood splintered and gave way, shattered by the powerful blows of the metal arm.

This was the moment that Sakura had been prompted to wait for; now she urged the children to start sending out powerful suggestions to all the delegates.

"Stop this madman! Seek peace with your fellowmen! Confess your crimes while you can!"

They sent this message out to everyone in the auditorium, over and over again. The message drummed in their ears, in their skulls; there was nothing else but these words in the whole of creation! How could they resist this command? To resist was to invite pain such as they had never known before... pain screamed inside their heads; agree, surrender, confess!

Yet some resisted. For four minutes they resisted the awful commands; noses started to bleed, blood ran from their scalps and mixed with the blood that was already seeping from their eye sockets; blood spilled everywhere, they couldn't see, couldn't hear, couldn't taste anything else; only blood, their blood!

Some collapsed; others tried to run, but fell as their brains began to haemorrhage blood; yet a few stopped fighting the command. They knelt in surrender and confessed their sins; they agreed to reform their corrupt regimes, and so found release and absolution.

When it was all over, there was blood splashed everywhere, on the carpets and the delegates' consoles; it was as if someone had sprayed blood from a hose high into the air.

Long Wei lay in a pool of his own blood, but his prosthetic half still twitched. Jim Stewart walked down to the dais. He stood over the body of Long Wei. His cybernetic brain tried to mouth some words but it was unable to form them. Jim pressed the descanners together; the machine brain died and the limbs ceased twitching.

Ian McGregor, Francois Bernard and Herschel Schwartz lay comatose on the floor, not dead but severely injured.

"Daddy, what will become of these men?" little Grace asked.

"Gracie, they will face justice for their crimes. May their victims show more mercy to them than they did to everyone! It will take a little time, but there has to be a cleansing of society, so that the new world order may grow. People like you will one day be everywhere, and this must never happen again!"

Chapter Twenty-Nine: A Telepathic World

It changed everything. To be sure, the events of May the First at the LCCC changed the world political blocs; the leader of the E.A.R. was eliminated and the three dictators of the Euro Zone were exposed, disgraced and detained pending formal charges to be filed for a court trial at the European Court of Justice; but a profoundly more fundamental change to society had begun a week earlier.

With the introduction of synthetic KP into the water supply reservoirs of the world's major cities, an irreversible process was put into motion, as Field Marshal David Miller had prophesied. First, individuals began to be aware; not self-awareness, which had always been a trait of humanity; but becoming aware of the thoughts, feelings and perhaps the unexpressed intentions of others around them; that was something new.

From individuals, the awareness spread to communities, and then to citywide awareness. It soon became known that by exercising and stretching the gift, as with all abilities, the latent telepathic ability could increase; this was particularly evident in children and young adults. Being aware of the thoughts of others, and knowing that one's own thoughts were broadcasting to the neighbourhood, lead to a change in personal thoughts and then to changes in behaviour.

For example, a person suspected of criminal acts would appear before a senior police officer. If that policeman had telepathic abilities, he could establish that the suspect was lying about his guilt, because his thoughts were declaring that he was in fact guilty. But the law of any country did not permit one to be convicted on the basis of one's thoughts' confession; the law required that evidence be produced, either physical or sometimes circumstantial, that would enable a jury to decide on the basis of that evidence. Or, if there was a 'reasonable doubt', then the court had to dismiss the charges, or in some jurisdictions to reach a finding of 'not proven'. Thus the law made no provision for telepathic knowledge.

Therefore, if there was now a proven evidence of telepathic ability, should not the law be amended? And what weight should the judge give to telepathic evidence? These and related issues had to be debated in the government assemblies of the world; not least because of the huge number of ordinary criminals who were literally begging now for judgment because of the torment that awareness had brought them to; the families of victims of violent crime being aware that the perpetrator of the crime was now 'confessing' insisted that justice be brought to bear on the basis of his declared thoughts. One of the fundamental Judeo-Christian principles of law is that every case must be established by the testimony of two or more witnesses. This principle is embodied in most legal systems today.

Legislators had to decide whether one of the two witnesses could be the person himself; but this was generally agreed to be unsafe, because if, say, the accusing police officer had a bias and made a false evidence of a telepathic confession, then his testimony would be uncorroborated.

Eventually the legislators agreed that; each higher court would include two judges with telepathic ability; in the case of a 'guilty' plea, the court would not rely upon physical evidence for a conviction, but corroboration from the accused would suffice; in the case of a 'not guilty' plea, the physical evidence would have equal weight with the telepathic findings of a court expert witness; and the two telepaths sitting as judges would have to confirm the telepathic confession.

Such fundamental changes in the Law might have been expected to take long, but surprisingly the weight of opinion favoured the telepathic factor and changes to the codes of practice of the law courts were rushed through in a little over a year.

For the high profile cases, such as the triumvirate of the Euro Zone, the changes in the law of Euro Zone were extremely bad news; they knew that their public humiliation was a foregone conclusion, since they couldn't stop broadcasting their memories of atrocities and judicial murders of their rivals. With each new 'confession' another investigation would be launched and more evidence was sure to come to light; their power previously had rested in their ability to control public information, but now public information was going to control them!

Immediately following the ratification of the 'telepathy law', as it came to be called, the Euro Zone High Court asked for a list of charges to be presented against the three defendants. The lists were very long; the major indictments included embezzlement of public funds, misuse of public office, theft, human trafficking, slavery, murder and treason. Under European law, the death penalty had been abolished for all crimes, save for the crime of treason; thus it was to be the main focus of the prosecution, but the worst case scenario would ensure that none of the three would ever see freedom again, because the number of indictments for each of them went into triple figures on the lesser charges just listed.

McGregor, Bernard and Schwartz knew that their death sentences rested on the testimony of Yuri Galenko, with the recorded conversation that damned McGregor, but also on the telepathically-obtained confessions of guilt for their endangerment of the Euro Zone in exchange for promises of cheap energy deals for the Russian Federation. They all decided to plead guilty.

Unusually, King Charles the Fourth of Britain appealed for the execution of Ian McGregor to be carried out in London, and the court agreed that each prisoner might be extradited to their home country to be executed in the manner chosen by that country's laws.

Ian McGregor was sentenced to die by public hanging at a specially prepared site in Hyde Park, London Central. The British Government also decreed that while in custody, until his hanging he was to be held incommunicado.

The date for his execution was fixed as November the Fifth, which seemed fitting as it commemorated the execution of another traitor, Guy Fawkes, who in 1605 tried to blow up the English Houses of Parliament. McGregor had also tried to destroy democracy but he was at least to be spared being tortured, drawn and quartered before being hanged.

The Fifth of November was to be henceforth a public holiday in England. The preciousness of their liberty had been forgotten and the day had become a time for parties and bonfires, but with the execution of McGregor a reawakening of national identity occurred, which may have been the King's intent all along.

A public hanging is a sad and pathetic end for any human being. It was a brutalized person that would derive any pleasure from watching a 'dead man's dance' at the end of a rope; yet, among the huge crowd that turned out to see the diminutive Scotsman paraded before mounting the scaffold, there were quite a few who cheered at his demise.

Ian McGregor, who was once a proud man, boastful and arrogant, wept pathetically as he was half-carried up the steps of the scaffold platform. Gone was the old self-made man in his expensive hand-tailored suits and shoes; what stood quivering on the platform was a pathetic, wasted shell.

As the rope snapped his neck, the crowd was silent. The dreadful finality of that moment would be etched into every mind, because of the enhancement by KP that gave everybody the shared experience of his terror and shame; right until he dropped down onto the hangman's noose.

McGregor's partners fared a little better; their governments, appalled at the public execution of McGregor and the unpredicted mental trauma to the onlookers, decided to carry out their executions in privacy. The actual events were captured on video, which was then entered into the public archives.

Each country decided what was in the best public interest; the majority followed the Franco-German model in the hope that the wounds of the past would thereby heal quicker.

However, in the E.A.R., a decision was made that the most senior members of the Wei Regime who had been found guilty of the most serious crimes, were to be executed by their victims' surviving relatives, whose names were selected randomly from the list. The mode of execution was reverted to the ancient tradition of execution by sword; the sword was wielded by the relative of a victim, and usually it only took one or two attempts to sever the head from the neck.

The international community cooperated fully in the hunt for those who fled the jurisdiction where their crimes had been registered. One such was Wolf Braun. He was pursued across several borders, but always managed to elude capture; but fate was against him. He had fled into hiding in the Ural Mountains, which was a region that he knew well, having travelled extensively about the mountains and towns to hunt his quarries; those whom he executed had been marked as 'Enemies of the State' by the Euro Zone Security Department. His reason for choosing the area now was that, because it was a rural region, there was less likelihood of the water supply containing the synthetic KP, so the citizens most probably were drinking natural ground water from wells and springs; which was true, for they did so. Therefore, he was less likely to run across a telepath.

Wolf decided to hide out at a mountain skiing resort called Gora Volchikha, which was forty kilometres west of the closest small town that was called Revda. It was not a well-known resort, and sufficiently remote that visitors usually gave it a miss. In the summertime, the slope was closed, and there were no chair lifts or trails for trekking, so it was not inviting for visitors; only locals came there. Even in the wintertime, it was almost deserted. The largest resort in the area was called Gora Belaya, and in spite of the regional government's big investment in a hotel, restaurants, saunas and a swimming pool, that resort too was deserted most of the year.

Wolf decided that he would spend most of his time in the smaller resort of Gora Volchikha where he camped and trekked about the mountains, and occasionally he would stop at the hotel in Gora Belaya for some creature comforts. He posed as a retired teacher from Yekaterinburg, which was one of the largest cities in the Urals. It seemed the perfect hiding place. He spoke fluent Russian; however, it was not in the local dialect; but considering his alleged profession, this would not be surprising. So Wolf Braun planned that he would hunt game and fish from the rivers for as long as it would take, until the heat was off for his capture.

One evening, when he was staying at the hotel in Gora Belaya, he visited the hotel bar for a beer, as he was dry from the heat of a hot summer's day. He sat alone as always and avoided conversations with the locals; which, had he but known it, marked him out as an oddball in that close knit community.

One evening, he noticed one of the bar customers looking at him somewhat intently; and then turning to his neighbour, the man spoke quietly. Then the other man left the bar quickly. Wolf's hair at the nape of his neck began to bristle. He had been recognised!

He casually rose as if to leave, but the stranger smiled and shook his head; then he slowly lifted an antique hunting rifle and laid it across the bar top. The rifle was angled so that it could be directed at Wolf in a split second. Even for a skilled assassin like Wolf, it was impossible to cross the space between them fast enough. It was over!

It was moments later that the local policemen arrived and arrested Wolf. It turned out that they were there in force that night because of reports that a stranger had been hanging around the district for a few months now and the locals thought it suspicious; but it was pure chance that, that very night, a victim's brother happened to visit the village and recognised the man who had killed his brother ten years ago in Chelyabinsk. So the great assassin who had eluded highly skilled police trackers for a year was caught in the end by chance.

Wolf was extradited to the European Court of Justice where he was immediately put on trial and then transferred back to Germany where he was subsequently executed.

The hunt for the remaining fugitives continues even today and there will be no let up while there are still grieving relatives of victims to be placated; only justice will satisfy them. The severe punishment for those who abused their authority and took the law into their own hands is a warning to any who might be tempted to do suchlike again.

Telepathy will not prevent crime, if the perpetrators are inured to the consequences of public knowledge of their deeds; it can only sound a warning to the community who must act to uphold the force of law.

Chapter-Thirty: New Beginnings

Dr Jim Stewart waited on the platform of Castle Cary Railway Station. The Exeter Express Maglev train was due in shortly. It was a fine morning in May.

Exactly two years had passed since the events of the World Council Conference, but with the toppling of corrupt regimes that followed the LCCC bloodbath, changes for the better were becoming visible at the grassroots level. The major effect in Britain and throughout the Euro Zone, in fact, was the removal of that climate of fear; people didn't have to go around fearing that the hand of the Defenders might suddenly descend upon their shoulders, and they would be removed from society 'for enquiries', never to be seen again. Quite how many disappeared in this way during the twenty-year regime of Ian McGregor and John Sanford was not known, but hundreds of thousands would probably not be an exaggeration.

The other positive influence was undoubtedly the universal introduction of KP, which brought about social awareness, which in turn tended to inhibit crime.

Continual ingestion of the synthetic KP in fact consolidated the benefits of the initial dosing of the water supply, but now pressure was mounting for embryonic treatments to begin. While the children had latent abilities in genetics from their grandparents, Toshio and Glenda, they had not as yet begun the first steps to put into practice their knowledge. What was needed was Dr Glenda herself to share the results of her latest research and development of the techniques that she and Toshio had pioneered and to lead the new team.

This was the reason that Dr Jim was waiting for the Express on a fine May morning; Glenda was coming. It was with great difficulty that the whole tribe had been prevented from descending upon the station for her welcome; Jim reasoned that she would be better able to adjust to the excitement of the children, now six year olds, once she reached the farm. Besides, the ground car and rotor vehicles couldn't possibly carry everyone plus her baggage. Jim instructed the robotic porter to carry the bags of his visitor to the ground car and he would go ahead with Dr Glenda Woods in the rotor vehicle.

The third reason was a surprise, actually two; he had thought it fitting that they should honour the memory of his dear friend and her late husband with a short memorial service. Jim had purchased and imported an original Shinto Temple bell, which came from an old temple in the Kyoto area which had been destroyed by the E.A.R. invaders of Japan as part of their programme to destroy anything that was culturally exclusive to Japan.

The Maglev train silently rounded the long bend before Castle Cary Station; one never got used to the silence of the Maglev trains, as they whisked along the rails. Except for the occasional mournful wail of the klaxon horn, they passed through the countryside like ghosts; a testimony to the excellence of German technology and engineering.

The train slowed just as silently as it entered the station. One might never guess that only minutes before, this express was reaching speeds of two hundred and fifty kilometres per hour; but now, just as effortlessly, it glided to a halt.

Only five passengers alighted from the train, but Dr Glenda Woods would have stood out even had there been fifty disembarking passengers. She was tall, at one point seven metres, with intense blue eyes and brown hair. At fifty-five years old, she was still apt to turn heads; Jim could see where Sakura got her good looks from.

Jim waved and she stepped smartly along the platform and embraced Jim with a bear hug and a peck on the cheek.

"Jim, we meet again! But Sakura says that you don't remember me from the Hospital in Incheon. I ought to be downright offended. What do you say?" Her accent was a soft mid-western drawl and her eyes twinkled because she was teasing Jim.

Jim responded, "Lady, I'd have to have been drugged to forget you!" They both laughed easily; they were going to be good friends, you could tell.

"OK, Porter, see those bags with the red tags? You place them in the ground car which I showed you before and the auto-driver will know where to take them."

"Yes, sir," the Porter intoned, "I shall do it right away." With that, the robot rolled along the platform to collect the large pile of bags that had travelled with Glenda from Japan.

Jim and Glenda walked to his Rotor vehicle, which stood waiting on the helipad. "I shall give you the royal tour also as we are on the way, seeing that you are an American tourist, and we haven't seen any in these parts in many a long year!"

Glenda replied with a curtsey and a smile, "Why, thank you kindly, Jim! The children have been telling me all about the things to see down here, I'm looking forward to going for walks about the farm and the district. I really miss the girls and the kids, it's been nothing but work ever since Toshio died." A sad look flitted across her face, and then she smiled again, "You know that with children there are no secrets, especially these three! I know about the cherry trees that you planted at the farm! Akemi says that they are in full blossom now, it will be just like it was in Kyoto, before they came!"

"Don't worry," Jim replied, "I've heard that already the E.A.R. is entering into talks with some of the 'provinces' to restore full sovereignty to them. It will be a chance to rebuild Kyoto and all of the other places that they shattered."

The autopilot guided them on the circuitous route that Jim had programmed in and they flew over Priddy Village and the Circles. Jim showed Glenda how they evaded the assassins when they came to the caves.

Finally, they came to the farm where everyone was waiting to welcome her. The children jumped up and down, singing a little Japanese welcome song, and there were lots of hugs and kisses for everyone. Jim introduced his brothers Bill and John, and then they all went inside. Glenda was tired after her long journey, so it was agreed that tomorrow they would allow the children to conduct her on a complete tour of the farm. She was especially interested to see the laboratory which Jim had, with Sakura's technical advice, fitted out for medical research and genetic testing.

"Do you know what the day after tomorrow is, Glenda? It is the third year Matsuri, seventh day." Jim continued, "With your permission, I would like to honour Toshio with a Matsuri memorial!"

"Oh, Jim," Glenda smiled at him through her tears, "What a dear, dear man you are!"

That evening, Jim, Bill and John went for a walk about the farm. Their path led them along the stream where Sakura and Jim had first kissed. The catkins had mostly finished now; soon it would be summer and other flowers would put forth along the streambed and in the woods nearby. Summer, autumn, winter and then spring again; there is a cycle to all things.

Jim wanted to talk with his brothers away from the family about what he had planned for Toshio's memorial. He decided to begin by explaining a little about the Shinto faith.

"Shinto is the indigenous religion of Japan. The other main religion is a form of Buddhism. Shinto is primarily animistic; it has no real founder or any written scriptures. The followers of the Shinto believe that humans are basically good by nature, but they do worship deities such as Amaterasu, the

Sun Goddess, who is believed to be the ancestress of the Imperial Family. In Shintoism, one's ancestors are highly revered, and they too are worshipped. We shall not be able to have a proper funeral for Toshio, because his body was taken away by the soldiers of General Chi; that was a most cruel act to a Shinto family."

"It is the custom in Japan to plan every element of a funeral carefully and there is a sequence of anniversaries that has to be observed also. There is a memorial stone erected for the deceased parent, and great care is taken in the upkeep of the gravesites and the home shrines. Normally, the ashes of the parent are interred under the memorial stone at the gravesite, and usually fresh flowers are brought weekly, and at each visit prayers are said with the burning of incense."

"In a devout Shinto family there will be a family shrine also where daily prayers will be said each morning, and incense, food and drink are offered to their ancestors. Great reverence is held for every element of the remembrance. The dishes and flower vases have to be cleaned each morning, and even before the family meals are prepared these rituals are carried out."

"It is a characteristic of the Shinto ceremonies that great care is taken in preparation. There is a precise protocol to be followed, which has been established for centuries-old protocols. There are over twenty procedures involved in an actual burial, but we shall be observing a memorial, as I said earlier, so there will be no Shinto priest officiating. Four of the main procedures are named; kichu-fuda, koden, kotsuage, and bunkotsu. Kichu-fuda is a period of intense mourning, which lasts for one day. Today, the Hokaida clan will be observing this procedure, so I figured that it would be best if we let them have a time alone for this. During the day of mourning, family and friends give an obituary gift; this is known as Koden. Koden is given to help defray the costs of the funeral expenses, but I shall bear these costs myself."

"I am not sure whether General Chi would have returned Toshio's ashes to the family; probably not, but if so, then the next procedure is the gathering of a person's ashes. This is known as Kotsuage. The ashes are placed in an urn, which is buried at the gravesite. The fourth of the major stages is the Bunkotsu procedure; in this stage some ashes are given to close family members, who will keep them in their home shrines."

"These ceremonies are very important in Shintoism; and every part of the burial ceremony has to be done in a certain way and at a certain time. The memory of their ancestors is kept alive because of the daily rituals of prayers and offerings at the family shrine. Now of particular significance to us is the observance of the anniversary; ceremonies actually are held on the first, third, seventh, thirteenth, and thirty-third years following the death of a beloved. There is an anniversary tradition called Matsuri which takes place on the third, seventh, and forty ninth days of these anniversary years. As I mentioned to Glenda, tomorrow is the Matsuri seventh day of the third year after Toshio's death, so I thought that it would be fitting to give Toshio a proper memorial now that the family is gathered together again in a time of peace and while the cherry blossoms are blooming."

"Incidentally Bill, would you please take the Rotor vehicle up to Bristol International Airport tonight? I have arranged for the Hokaida cousins' parents to join us. They were in America as refugees, but now wish to return home and this is sort of on the way!"

"I have to do some things today to arrange for the memorial service; and, oh, by the way, after the memorial there will be another short ceremony; Sakura and I are going to get married!"

The brother looked at each other and laughed. Jim looked at them, puzzled at their reaction. "What's up with you guys, you don't think I should marry her? I know she is a lot younger than me, but well, we just seem to suit each other!"

"No, Jim," John assured him, "it's just that, well, we were going to tell you today… you aren't the only one who's getting married! We hadn't fixed a day yet, but Bill and I have both popped the question and Asuka and Ren have both said yes! Why don't we make it a triple wedding? I am sure that the ladies would love it too."

Without further ado, John picked up his comm. link and spoke to Ren; then he passed it to Bill, who spoke for a while and then nodded to his brothers. "She says that normally they have to observe a thirty day mourning period after a death, but they all agreed that since this is a memorial

235

ceremony and we have entered a new era in a new country, it would be alright to make a new beginning after we have honoured Toshio."

"OK then; let me see if I can get someone to come up from the Cathedral in Wells to officiate," Jim replied, "it's short notice, but maybe if I offer to repair their roof or something that might swing it!"

Chapter Thirty-One: In Memoriam

A small group stood before the avenue of cherry trees. The sun shone and a light spring breeze stirred the leaves. Cherry blossoms blew down upon them like pink and white snow flurries.

The memorial service was brief but poignant. Jim thanked everyone for coming and then handed the ceremony over to Toshio's brother, Toshiaki. As the senior surviving relative, it was Toshiaki's responsibility to conduct the farewell ceremony. Toshiaki was so much alike his brother, it was hard to believe looking at him that Toshio was really gone; his mannerisms were the same, even the voice inflections reminded Jim of his dead friend. A tear started to roll down Jim's cheek but Sakura noticed and caught it.

"For luck!" she whispered.

Toshiaki spoke in Japanese of Toshio; what an honourable man he was, how brave too; a hero in Korea where he saved many lives, in the war field as well as in the hospital wards. He glanced at Jim as he spoke these words. He spoke of his patriotism and his bravery in defending his wife, daughter and granddaughter against the men who invaded his home in Kyoto; although outnumbered, he was defeating the E.A.R. soldiers until a coward, General Chi, stole up behind Toshio and stabbed him in the back. In his brave resistance, he secured time enough for his family to escape the soldiers, and for his wife, Dr Glenda Woods, to carry on the legacy of their joint research. Their work had changed the world; it was fitting that a memorial should be held in this foreign country with emblems of Japan floating on the morning breeze about his memorial stone.

Next, Dr Glenda spoke a few words, in Japanese and English. She spoke of the dashing young scientist that won her heart on the battlefields of Korea; how he was so intense and passionate about his work in genetics, and how much he loved his home city of Kyoto. She spoke of hope for the future, which was built upon the work of Toshio, who she credited with the initial discovery of KP. Together in life they had been inseparable; Toshio left a void that no one else would ever be able to fill.

Sakura spoke for herself and Grace; how Toshio was a father who wore his heart on his sleeve. Even when he was busy, he somehow found time to play with baby Grace and be a father to her, even though Sakura was considered an outcast in the community because she had borne an illegitimate child. No one could be told about the reason that she, Asuka and Ren had to endure such shame and rejection. It was a sacrifice for Toshio also; for his part he had to bear the pain of rejection by his friends for the shame of an unmarried daughter with child.

Each of the party then laid a flower before the simple granite stone that Jim had had erected for Toshio, and as they returned, they swung the huge horizontal clapper beam twice that sounded the

Shinto bell across the Mendip Hills. They all stood then for a minute's silence.

Then Jim with Sakura, Bill with Asuka, and John with Ren formed a half-circle before the Rector who had come up from Wells to conduct the marriage vows. The ceremony took about forty minutes as three brothers and their three brides joined in wedlock, there amidst the falling cherry tree blossoms. Jim took Sakura's hand and they kissed.

"It was meant to be!" he said.

Glossary of terms

Akemi: a Japanese female name which means 'bright beauty'.

Akiyoshi: a Japanese male name which means 'bright and good'.

Artificial Intelligenc (AI): Ability of a machine to perform tasks thought to require human intelligence. Typical applications include game playing, language translation, expert systems, and robotics. Although pseudo-intelligent machinery dates back to antiquity, the first glimmerings of true intelligence awaited the development of digital computers in the 1940s. AI, or at least the semblance of intelligence, has developed in parallel with computer processing power, which appears to be the main limiting factor. Early AI projects, such as playing chess and solving mathematical problems, are now seen as trivial compared to visual pattern recognition, complex decision making, and the use of natural language. Sourced from; Britannica Concise Encyclopedia

Asuka: a Japanese female name which means 'tomorrow fragrance'

Bionic: A machine that is patterned after principles found in humans or nature; for example, robots. It also refers to artificial devices implanted into humans replacing or extending normal human functions. Source; answers.com/topic/bionic

Brain-machine interface: brain machine interface (BRI) enables a person's brain to accept a mechanical device as part of its representation of the human body and allows the person to control the device just by thinking. Brain machine interfaces read signals from neurons and use computers and algorithms to translate those signals into action. The immediate goal of these interfaces is to enable people with damaged sensory and motor functions to control devices with their brains. Thus, for example, in the future, paraplegics may be able to control motorized wheelchairs just by thinking, or amputees might be able to move artificial limbs with just their thoughts. The earliest interfaces developed in this breakthrough field of research require scientists to insert electrodes into the skull in order to physically tap directly into the brain, and researchers are currently trying to develop technologies that will enable them to access neurological activity through minimally invasive techniques. It is hoped that someday brain machine interfaces will be able to read neural signals non-invasively, from outside the skull, and that devices will be operated involuntarily, without deliberate conscious thought. Thus, for example, fighter pilots wearing specialized helmets may be able to operate some controls automatically, just by thinking. Source; answers.com/topic/brain-machine-interface

241

Cold fusion; Cold fusion refers to a proposed nuclear fusion process offered to explain a group of disputed experimental results first reported by electrochemists Martin Fleischmann and Stanley Pons. Proponents may prefer "Low Energy Nuclear Reaction" (LENR) or "Chemically Assisted Nuclear Reaction" (CANR) to avoid the negative connotations associated with the original name. The field originates with reports of an experiment by Martin Fleischmann, then one of the world's leading electrochemists, and Stanley Pons in March 1989 where they reported anomalous heat production ("excess heat") of a magnitude they asserted would defy explanation except in terms of nuclear processes. They further reported measuring small amounts of nuclear reaction by-products, including neutrons and tritium. The small tabletop experiment involved electrolysis of heavy water on the surface of a palladium (Pd) electrode.

The media reported that nuclear fusion was happening inside the electrolysis cells, and these reports raised hopes of a cheap and abundant source of energy. Hopes fell when replication failures were weighed, in view of several reasons cold fusion is not likely to occur, the discovery of possible sources of experimental error, and finally the discovery that Fleischmann and Pons had not actually detected nuclear reaction by-products. By late 1989, most scientists considered cold fusion claims dead, and cold fusion subsequently gained a reputation as pathological science. In 1989, the majority of a review panel organized by the US Department of Energy (DOE) found that the evidence for the discovery of a new nuclear process was not persuasive enough to start a special program, but was "sympathetic toward modest support" for experiments "within the present funding system." A second DOE review, which was convened in 2004 to look at new research, reached conclusions similar to the first.

A small community of researchers continues to investigate cold fusion, claiming to replicate Fleischmann and Pons' results including nuclear reaction by-products. These claims are largely disbelieved in the mainstream scientific community. Source; Wikipedia

Cybernetics: Cybernetics comes from a Greek word meaning "the art of steering". Practitioners of cybernetics use models of organizations, feedback, goals, and conversation to understand the capacity and limits of any system (technological, biological, or social); they consider powerful descriptions as the most important result; knowing whether you have reached your goal (or at least are getting closer to it) requires "feedback", a concept that comes from cybernetics. From the Greek, "cybernetics" evolved into Latin as "governor"; sourced from-pangaro.com/published/ cyber-macmillan.html

EMP: Electromagnetic Pulse. The way that EMP works is that a source generates an electric field whose gradient is so strong that extremely high voltages are actually generated between two different points in free space. Present technology does not generate sufficient power in a hand held device. The author considers that a hundred years from now this might be feasible.

Fuel Cell: Device that converts chemical energy of a fuel directly into electricity. Fuel cells are intrinsically more efficient than most other energy-conversion devices. Electrolytic chemical reactions cause electrons to be released on one electrode and flow through an external circuit to a second electrode. Whereas in batteries the electrodes are the source of the active ingredients, which are altered and depleted during the reaction, in fuel cells the gas or liquid fuel (often hydrogen, methyl alcohol, hydrazine, or a simple hydrocarbon) is supplied continuously to one electrode and oxygen or air to the other from an external source. So, as long as fuel and oxidant are supplied, the fuel cell will not run down or require recharging. Fuel cells can be used in place of virtually any other source of electricity. They are especially being developed for use in electric automobiles, in the hope of achieving enormous reductions in pollution. Sourced from; Britannica Concise Encyclopedia

Grace: a female name which means 'unmerited favour from God'.

Ground car: a fictional vehicle powered by a chemically powered propulsion unit and electric fuel cells.

Glenda: a female name which means 'fair, good, literary'.

Hu Wei: a Chinese male name which means 'tiger greatness'.

Long Wei: a Chinese male name which means 'dragon greatness'.

Maglev train: Magnetic levitation, maglev, or magnetic suspension is a method by which an object is suspended with no support other than magnetic fields. Magnetic pressure is used to counteract the effects of the gravitational and any other accelerations. In some cases the lifting force is provided by magnetic levitation, but there is a mechanical support bearing little load that provides stability. This is termed pseudo-levitation. Magnetic levitation is used for maglev trains, magnetic bearings and for product display purposes. – source; Wikipedia

Positronic: A positronic brain is a fictional technological device, originally conceived by science fiction writer Isaac Asimov. Its role is to serve as a central computer for a robot, and, in some unspecified way, to provide it with a form of consciousness recognizable to humans. When Asimov wrote his first robot stories in 1939/1940, the positron was a newly discovered particle and so the buzzword positronic, coined by analogy with electronic, added a contemporary gloss of popular science to the concept. Source; answers.com/topic/positronic-brain

Prosthesis: In medicine, a prosthesis, prosthetic, or prosthetic limb (Greek; πρόσθεσις "addition") is an artificial device extension that replaces a missing body part. It is part of the field of biomechatronics, the science of using mechanical devices with human muscle, skeleton, and nervous systems to assist or enhance motor control lost by trauma, disease, or defect. Prostheses are typically used to replace parts lost by injury (traumatic) or missing from birth (congenital) or to supplement defective body parts. Sourced from; answers.com

Ren: A Japanese female name which means 'water lily'.

RFID: A radio frequency identification tag (RFID) listens for a radio frequency and responds by transmitting a unique ID, typically a 64-bit identifier yielding 18,000 trillion possible values. A RFID tag may be a device that is implanted under the skin so that the bearer will be automatically identified when going to a checkout in a supermarket or an ATM cash machine, or in place of using a credit card. Initial research was undertaken at IBM and Texas Instruments. The device is marketed by Applied Digital Solutions (ADS) of Florida, USA. The ADS device measures 12 x 2.1 mm and is implanted under the skin by syringe using only a topical anaesthetic. The service is called VeriPay. Mastercard has been testing a similar RFID device called PayPass. Most RFID tags have no batteries but use the power from the initial radio frequency to transmit their response. This is the system used by Dubai, UAE in its SALIK road toll system, where a passive tag is mounted on the windscreen and the toll is automatically deducted from the account of the subscriber as the car passes in front of the tollgate transmitter.

Some systems of implanted device are capable of being monitored by Global Positioning Satellite (GPS) and can be powered by a small solar-rechargeable lithium-ion battery. The position of the bearer is therefore known in real time positioning. These devices may also be used to inject miniscule amounts of powerful psychotropic drugs that will control the personality or behaviour of the bearer from a remote location. Researchers have concluded that the optimum position for this type of device is the back of the right hand or on the forehead; the so-called 'mark of the beast'. The slogan of VeriChip Corporation says, "Trust us, it's for your own protection"; what they fail to mention is that control over all your finances will rest in the hands of the bankers. They will give the power to buy or sell and this may be refused at any moment by whoever controls the microchip.

Rotor/ Rotor Turbo vehicle: a fictional device using modified helicopter blades and a drive mechanism that is more efficient than a conventional helicopter's today.

Sakura: A Japanese female name which means 'cherry blossom'.

Thames Barrier: A Thames Barrier flood defence closure is triggered when a combination of high tides forecast in the North Sea and high river flows at the tidal limit at Teddington weir indicate that water levels would exceed 4.87 metres (16.0 ft) in central London. The flood defence closure begins with messages to stop river traffic, close subsidiary gates and alert other river users. As well as the Thames Barrier, the smaller gates along the Thames Tideway include Barking Barrier, King George V Lock gate, Dartford Barrier and gates at Tilbury Docks and Canvey Island. If the barrier was not there, the high tide would fill up this volume instead, and the floodwater could then spill over the river banks in London. In the 1980's there were four closures, 35 closures in the 1990's, and 75 closures in the first decade of this century. The barrier was closed twice on 9 November 2007 after a storm surge in the North Sea which was compared to the one in 1953. The barrier was originally designed to protect London against a big flood level, with a return period of one-thousand years up to the year 2030, after which the protection would decrease, whilst remaining within acceptable limits. Despite global warming and a consequently greater predicted rate of sea level rise, recent analysis extended the working life of the barrier until around 2060–2070. From 1982 until 19 March 2007, the barrier was raised one-hundred times to prevent flooding. Source; Wikipedia

Toshio: A Japanese male name which means 'bright, brilliant man".

Toshiaki: A Japanese male name which means 'bright, alert, happy'.

Urals: Urals or Ural Mountains, E European Russia and NW Kazakhstan, forming, together with the Ural River, the traditional boundary between Europe and Asia and separating the Russian plain from the W. Siberian lowlands. The population consists primarily of Russians, with some Bashkirs, Tatars, Udmurts, and Komi-Permyaks. Source; The Columbian Electronic Encyclopedia, Sixth Edition 2011.

Roger G. Trow

Roger lives with his wife Eleanor-Mary in Dubai, United Arab Emirates. In his career as a chartered land surveyor, he has travelled widely and worked overseas for almost forty years. He is co-founder with his wife of an award winning charity called Helpinghandsuae which deals with the needs of the migrant labour force in the UAE. Roger also enjoys cooking and social activities including prison visiting.